Other Authored Books

Service Starts With a Smile

Customer Service Superstars

Five-Star Service

Winning the Customer

Luxury Service

67 Life Applications
(Found in a Golf Lesson)

People Skills

Books may be purchased at:
www.carycavittconsulting.com

What fellow PGA Professionals are saying after a Service That Attracts Seminar™...

"A tremendous amount of good information that is immediately applicable to my operation. Great job Cary!"

"Great seminar with helpful information on customer service!"

"What I learned today will enhance my staff training this spring, creating greater service at my facility."

"Very enjoyable and enlightening. A good way to start the year."

"Great information and presented very well. I plan to use this information to not only improve my own customer service skills, but also share it with co-workers and enforce it upon summer staff and interns."

"I learned about the Yes Factor the hard way. Glad to know I'm doing many of these and was a good review and reminder of how to take care of my customers and relationships. Thanks!"

"Great speaker! Really got me to open my eyes to customer service. Outstanding seminar!"

"Great enthusiasm and educational. I would like my employees to experience Cary's presentation."

"I think Cary did a great job and gave us a lot of good points on how important it is that we treat our customers with respect and how we have to be friendly."

"The individual experiences with both poor and excellent customer service were enlightening. I can't wait to apply what I learned today."

"This seminar reminded me of the things that are important when dealing with customers and how to treat them."

"This presentation was very informative and open with discussion and stories. I'm glad I attended this customer service seminar and will use what I learned today for the rest of my life."

"Cary is a master at understanding and teaching service excellence. He has a unique ability to relate to and help all sorts of organizations truly improve their attitude towards client service."

Mr. Bob DiMeo
Managing Director
DiMeo Schneider & Associates
Founder – Golf Nation
www.golfnation.us

"Cary displays a unique commitment to people by his focus on personal service and satisfaction. Having watched Cary work with my sons over the years in his golf clinics, I learned that Cary's effect on people is much deeper."

Mr. Todd A. Rowden
Attorney-at-Law
Riffner - Barber - Rowden LLC
President, Palatine Rotary Club

An *Enjoyable* Golf Club Experience:

Offering every guest a friendly and cordial welcome by developing a well-trained golf staff who are dedicated to excellent service.

Table of Contents

Definition of a Golf Club:

Every golf facility, whether Private, Public, or Resort.

Definition of a Guest:

Every person (Member or Guest) who visits the Golf Club.

Introduction

The Tale of Two Golf Clubs

Once upon a time there were two Golf Clubs within the same town. Both were very similar in how well they maintained the course. The layouts of both courses were also very similar. Both were cut out of a large wooded forest area and were almost the same in terms of the overall challenge. The fairways and greens were manicured and the clubhouses were very comparable. Even the green fees were identical. By all outside appearances both Golf Clubs looked identical. But take a closer look and you will find a major difference in how guests rated their golfing experience at each facility.

The Green Forest Golf Club consistently was rated higher in golfer satisfaction than Hidden Woods Golf Club. Along with consistently given higher marks in voting surveys, Green Forest Golf Club consistently had more overall rounds. Not only was the bottom line always better at the end of the season, but they were never lacking on golfers wanting to join. On the other hand, Hidden Woods Golf Club struggled each season to reach their projected goals and never understood why they were always behind in rounds than Green Forest Golf Club. With similar accommodations and identical rates, they could never understand why their club was consistently ranked lower. Even though they practically matched Green Forest in almost every area, what they had failed to take into account *was the level of service that was provided.*

From the moment that guests arrived at the Green Forest Golf Club, they were given the immediate impression that the staff was glad to see them. Not only did each guest feel welcomed, but they also were given the impression that the staff at Green Forest truly wanted their experience to be as enjoyable as possible. Guests who played the Club consistently were telling others about their experience. Not only did they consistently return, but they also had become the Golf Club's best advertisement by telling others about their exceptional experience.

Every person on the staff at Green Forest Golf Club consistently maintained a friendly and service oriented attitude. *They understood the importance in their role in making the overall operation a success.* Each staff member had been fully trained to be aware of how important it was to treat the guest. They were consistent because they viewed each guest as a VIP. The staff also understood that in order to make Green Forest Golf Club successful, everyone must work together as a team in providing an exceptional experience for each guest who visited the club.

This was not the case at Hidden Woods Golf Club. Even though they offered a beautiful clubhouse and course, they sorely lacked when it came to providing an enjoyable experience for those who came to play. What Hidden Woods had failed to understand was the importance of creating a warm and inviting atmosphere for each guest. Not only did guests walk away feeling that the service was below average, but they also told others about their poor experience. What Hidden Woods Golf Club failed to understand was the importance of making their guests feel welcomed. They fail to understand the significance of being friendly and creating an inviting atmosphere. When guests were asked about their experience at Hidden Woods, they consistently commented on the unfriendliness of the staff. They also mentioned how they felt unappreciated as a guest.

As mentioned earlier, on all outside appearances both Clubs looked almost identical. *But what truly set them apart was the way that guests were treated.* Green Forest Golf Club understood the importance of making each guest feel welcomed and appreciated. On the other hand, Hidden Woods was oblivious on the importance of creating an inviting atmosphere for every guest. The reason they had never reached their potential as a Golf Club was because *they did not understand the importance of how to treat others*. They will only start to improve when they begin to realize the importance of treating their guests with friendliness, appreciation, and respect.

My hope is that each reader will begin to understand the importance in how we treat our guests and how this will ultimately be the measuring tool used in rating our facility. May we be to others what we would want for ourselves.

Best regards,

Cary Cavitt
PGA Professional

This book is dedicated to every PGA Member. May we continue to serve with professionalism, enthusiasm, and appreciation. Also, I would like to thank the PGA of America for its continual strong leadership.

Chapter 1
Make Every Guest Feel Welcomed
18 Reasons Why Guests Will Want to Return...

Let's start off with some basis ideas on what makes guests *want to return*. Remember that the key is to create an environment that not only attracts them back, but also gives them a legitimate reason to tell others about their experience. These 18 reasons are simple common sense ideas that will give us a starting point in offering an enjoyable experience for every guest who visits our facility.

Reason #1
Guests will return if you

Learn to smile more...

Our guests will feel more welcomed and at ease if we simply learn to greet them with a friendly smile.

Have you ever strolled into a Golf Club and felt comfortable right away? More than likely you were greeted with a friendly smile by one of the staff members who acknowledged you. It's amazing how a simple smile can make us automatically feel welcomed; yet how often we forget to give this powerful little gesture.

Golf Clubs that stress the importance of a smile when greeting others are ahead of their competition. The reason for this is that whenever we create a friendly environment for the guest, he or she will be drawn to return. The simple smile conveys to others that we are happy to see them and they in turn feel welcomed.

This powerful combination is really what guest service is all about. The more that we can make each guest feel comfortable, the more likely he or she will continue to come back to our facility. So remember to encourage your team to smile!

1

Reason #2
Guests will return if you

Simply ask yourself if you would enjoy being served by you…

Would you want to be served by you?

Here is a simple question to measure our guest service skills: Would you want to be served by you if you were the potential guest? If the answer is yes, then congratulations! But if you answered no, then consider ways to make others enjoy being served by you.

When we can put ourselves in another person's shoes and sincerely ask ourselves if we have served him or her to our best ability, then more than likely we would enjoy being served by ourselves. Consider the excellent guest service experiences that you have had in the past and try to pass on the memorable service to your guests.

In the end, when we simply ask ourselves if we would enjoy being served in the same manner, we can begin to improve and give others great guest service.

Reason #3
Guests will return if you

Make each guest feel welcomed...

When a club shows itself to be friendly and welcoming, guests will be drawn to return.

I believe that the number one factor in drawing people back as repeat guests is based on how well that *they feel* that they were treated. Notice that I said how *they* feel. In the majority of cases, many facilities honestly believe that they do an excellent job at making each guest feel welcomed. But in reality this is not the case.

Very rarely do we come across a club that truly goes the extra step in making sure that our experience during a visit is outstanding. Far too often I have heard stories about experiences that golfers have had at different golf facilities. I believe that many guests feel this way simply because they did not feel welcomed and appreciated.

So remember that the key to guests coming back is to treat them with a friendly welcome and appreciation for choosing our facility.

Reason #4
Guests will return if you
Hire the right people...

During the interview ask questions that will help to determine whether the candidate enjoys helping others.

Finding the right people for the team is the key to ultimate success. But how do we find the best candidate during the interviewing process? Here are two quick tips to watch for:

1. **Watch for great smiles.** Make sure that the candidate can easily smile. I recently went to a local school to volunteer to interview 8th graders who were being trained in writing resumes and interviewing techniques. After interviewing nine students, I chose the first candidate because of his easy-going smile. I felt right away that if he could easily smile in an interview, he could easily smile with guests as well.

2. **Do they enjoy serving others?** This is really the key. Be sure to get a sense of whether or not the possible candidate has a heart to serve. By asking the right questions and really listening to the responses, we should be able to get a fairly accurate reading into whether or not the candidate enjoys helping others.

Reason #5
Guests will return if you

Make the work environment enjoyable…

Happy staff members will always offer the best service.

As I have grown in my understanding of guest relationships, I have also come to realize that the intelligent management teams see each staff member as their best guest. Why have I come to this conclusion? It's really quite simple: *Happy staff members will always offer the best service.*

When management works toward making the work environment enjoyable, the staff members respond more positively to guests. The whole atmosphere changes for the better.

Gone are the days when managers ruled with an iron fist. The smart leaders have the ability to create a team that not only works well together but also laughs together. Study after study shows that guest service is greatly enhanced when staff members enjoy their work environment. This alone will do wonders for your Golf Club!

Reason #6
Guests will return if you

Give guests more than they expected…

Guests will walk away feeling that the experience was outstanding simply because we gave them more.

Every once in a while as guests we receive more than expected. When this occurs we automatically feel that the Golf Club was fair and trustworthy. Because *"they did not have to do it,"* we somehow feel obligated to them in a good way.

In essence, we appreciate what they did for us that we want to tell others about the experience. What happened in reality is that we feel that the club really cared about us. Smart Golf Clubs understand this basic principle. They will always try to go the extra mile in making sure that they exceed their guest's expectations. This alone can have a major impact simply because the vast majority of guests expect average service.

Remember this and you will find new golfers knocking on your door in no time. These guests will also be your best advertisers and tell their friends about the exceptional service!

Reason #7
Guests will return if you

Are attentive...

Being attentive always increases sales.

Sales will always increase when staff members are attentive to the guest in a non-pushy manner. This is because the guest feels that he or she is being treated as an important person. When the staff are attentive, they are letting every guest know that they are there for them. This alone has a powerful impact in the decision that the guest has in how well the club is measured.

On the other hand, when a Golf Club is slack in being attentive to others, it will soon find itself losing guests. People who take on the role of being a guest expect to be treated with attentiveness. That is one of the major attractions in going shopping. Many guests crave the shopping experience simply because others are attentive to them.

So remember this when training your staff. It is a small tip but results in more satisfied guests and better sales for your club.

Reason #8
Guests will return if you

Allow refunds...

Posting a NO RAINCHECKS sign up only makes guests less receptive to doing business with your Golf Club.

We have all come face-to-face with the dreaded NO RAINCHECKS or NO REFUNDS sign hanging near the register. This has to go down as one of the worst signs for creating guest loyalty.

Here is the reason why. First of all, guests will more than likely interpret this sign to read something like this:

"WE DO NOT CARE ABOUT YOUR SATISFACTION"
"YOU REALLY CANNOT TRUST US"
"WE'VE GOT YOUR MONEY NOW!"

Because the sign is usually next to the cash register, guests leave with a negative feeling. People will not return when they feel that they cannot trust the Golf Club. They automatically feel uncomfortable about making a purchase. But on the other hand, when the policy offers refunds, guests will feel more secure. This in turn increases sales and brings people back to your club.

Reason #9
Guests will return if you

Respond quickly...

Working quickly during peak guest hours will convey to them that we respect their time.

As guests, we all want to be served quickly. No one wants to wait for very long. This is especially true when lines begin to form. All we have to do is look at the faces. No one seems to be very happy waiting.

It is important that guests see that we are working quickly to take care of them as they are patiently waiting. When guests see that we are going as quickly as possible, it gives them the perception that we truly care.

This alone will give them a favorable impression when they are finally served and leaving the clubhouse. Inside they know that it is not our fault and appreciate the fact that we did our best to serve them.

On the other hand, I have witnessed the opposite effect where a staff member did not appear to work quickly as others were patiently waiting. This gave the impression that the guest was not important. This attitude will eventually have a negative effect on whether guests decide to return in the future.

Reason #10
Guests will return if you

Remember that they have many options…

Providing excellent service becomes more important when we realize that our guests have other options.

Gone are the days when the town had only one Golf Club. In the world of today the guest is given many options to choose from. If he or she does not like a particular club, he can take his pick from five other local courses. It's just like if another guest did not have an enjoyable experience at the new restaurant in town, she has nine similar restaurants to choose from.

This is why it is absolutely critical to win new guests by giving them the best service possible. Other clubs may be able to match our quality and price, but if we can have the best service in town it will be hard to lose guests.

As a Golf Club it is important for everyone to remember that guests have other options. If we can keep this in the back of our mind, we will focus more on giving outstanding service. And remember, guests are doing us a favor by walking through our doors when in fact they could have easily gone somewhere else.

Reason #11
Guests will return if you

Simply go the extra mile...

Most guests will be pleasantly surprised when we offer great service that was not expected.

For the most part, guests enter a Golf Club and expect average service. This is just a fact. They expect the service to be just the normal run of the mill.

The expectations of an average guest are actually quite low when it comes to being served at a club. The reason for this is because they have had so many experiences with average to below average service that they actually expect it from others.

This of course is a big advantage for your Golf Club if you understand this simple point. Your guests will be pleasantly surprised when you give them just a little extra service. They will be totally caught off guard by your positive attitude and sincere desire to serve them. They will walk away and want to tell others about their great experience.

Reason #12
Guests will return if you

Follow the golden rule of management...

Great managers always follow the golden rule of management.

Great managers all have a similar attribute that separates them from the pack. It is called the golden rule of management: "Treat every staff member the way you want every staff member to treat the guest."

The smart manager first and foremost creates an environment where each staff member at the Golf Club can grow as a person. A manager who sincerely cares for others and shows it in his or her actions shapes the atmosphere.

When the team is treated with respect and encouraged to use their gifts and abilities in an environment of mutual respect, everyone wins and the Golf Club begins to thrive. This simple rule will go a long way in building a better service team, cheerful employees, and guests who will want to return.

Reason #13
Guests will return if you

Have a friendly telephone voice...

Guests will automatically make a judgment of the service offered simply by the tone of voice that they hear.

The very first impression that every caller will make of your Golf Club is the tone of voice that is used on the telephone. The words used are not nearly as important as the tone that is heard by the caller.

A negative opinion of the Golf Club can be made if the caller senses that the team member who is answering the telephone is not responding to the questions in a friendly tone of voice.

On the other hand, when the team member projects a friendly attitude and reflects a patient tone of voice to the caller, the caller will have a positive opinion of the club.

Remember that showing patience and a friendly tone of voice will draw guests in and give them a great first impression of your overall operation. This alone will have a great influence on whether or not they will do business in the future.

Reason #14
Guests will return if you

Return telephone messages quickly...

Give guests a great first impression by promptly returning telephone messages.

How many times have you left a telephone message and did not receive a call back? It happens all the time. For some unexplainable reason returned telephone calls seldom happen in the business world.

When we promptly return a telephone message we are telling the guest that he or she is important. On the other hand, when a message is not returned it gives the impression that our Golf Club does not value guests. We must remember that they took the time to call and leave a message. It is only common courtesy that we honor this by returning their message.

The second reason in returning messages is that it reflects great service. The person who left the message will remember our prompt call back and think highly of the quick response. It will let them know that our Golf Club is on the ball and can be dependable in the future. This quick response will always reflect positively and give guests a reason to patronize our club.

Reason #15
Guests will return if you

Make doing business incredibly easy...

Serving our guests in a quick and efficient manner will always convey that we respect their time.

We all have had the experience of doing business with a Golf Club that was incredibly difficult. The transaction process was slow and we left with the feeling of never wanting to return. One easy way to give great service is to provide a simple and efficient transaction for every guest.

Let me share an example that will hit home. Let us say that every time we visit a local restaurant the waitresses are incredibly slow. So what happens? Eventually we find another restaurant.

Great service needs to respect the time of each guest. When a transaction is long and difficult, guests will eventually find another club to play.

It is important to train each staff member to finish transactions as quickly as possible and give guests the impression that their time is valuable. By doing this, they will always leave with an impression that the service was excellent.

15

Reason #16
Guests will return if you

Learn how to take care of complaints…

Listening and empathy will go a long way in calming down an upset guest.

Every staff member will eventually be confronted with an upset guest. There are some positive ways to handle this situation. The most important key is to actively listen to the complaint. Allow the guest to talk. This alone will show that we care.

It is important to maintain a calm voice when replying back if the guest is speaking in a louder than normal voice. Never raise your own voice. In these situations the guest is looking for two responses. The first is simply to be heard. The complaint may be legitimate and assist us in the future so that it is never repeated.

The second response that the guest is looking for is empathy. If we can show that we understand how he or she feels, we are then giving a thoughtful response. The upset guest will more than likely calm down simply because we have listened and showed empathy. Now it is our turn to handle and take care of the situation in a calm and professional manner.

Reason #17
Guests will return if you

Learn from other service superstars...

We will know that a service superstar has served us by their friendliness and the way that they have made us feel.

One of the fastest ways to learn how to be a service superstar is to observe our own experiences as a guest. Being on the other side of the counter will give us a different perspective.

I love to observe and watch how others treat me as a guest. Every so often I will come across a service superstar. They are courteous, attentive, and make me feel great to have done business with them. These superstars have a way of making me feel welcomed and appreciated. When we make a conscious effort to observe others, we will begin to recognize certain actions and attitudes that may or may not work.

Remember to keep your eyes open when you come across the superstars. You will recognize them by their smile and the way they make you feel. We can learn a lot from them.

Reason #18
Guests will return if you

Are genuinely happy
to see them…

*There is no better feeling of being greeted by someone who is
genuinely happy to see us.*

There is a secret in providing a great first impression for your guests
that works every time. This little secret only works when we mean it
from our heart.

So what is this great secret that will win guests? It is being genuinely
happy to see them. There is no better feeling of being greeted by
someone who is happy and honored to see us. We tend to perk up and
feel happy ourselves!

When others are glad to see us we feel a sense of belonging and this in
turns makes us feel more comfortable. Because the first few minutes
are crucial in the experience of a guest, it is important to be consistent
in providing a friendly greeting.

All of us enjoy the feeling that others are happy to see us. We long for
affirmation and the sense that people care. This will go a long way in
offering our guests a great service experience. Being genuinely happy
to see them provides a great first impression and a reason to return.
Mean it from the heart and watch what happens!

Chapter 2
It Starts With the Right Attitudes

6 Attitudes That Create Outstanding Service...

It has been said that attitude is everything when it comes to approaching the many challenges in life. How we view each day can be a reflection of the attitude that we carry with us. We can choose either to look at every situation with an attitude that will help or hinder us. It is our choice alone.

In the area of guest service it is no different. How we treat each guest is a reflection of the attitude that we bring with us to the job. Our attitude can assist or hold us back in providing the best possible service. That is why it is essential to understand that certain attitudes can make us guest service superstars if we will only learn to apply them into our lives.

Over the years I have found it quite fascinating how our inner attitudes can determine so much of how we view daily life. This is especially true in the area of serving guests. We can have all of the right training in how to treat others, but it will never quite work if we do not have the six attitudes that will be shared.

Since each of us can relate to what it feels like to be a guest, we will discover that the great memories we have personally had of being served well were in reality the result of being assisted by someone who had these qualities. On the other hand, we can all relate to moments as

19

a guest where we were treated rather poorly. This too can be tied in with being served by someone who simply lacked these six attitudes.

A famous 20th century writer once penned...

> *I have learned silence from the talkative, toleration from the intolerant, and kindness from the unkind, yet strange, I am ungrateful to those teachers.*

Each one of us has played the role of a guest in literally hundreds of different situations. Think of the countless experiences that we have all had of being a guest and the service that was provided to us.

I once read another quote that has never left me. It simply said:

> *"People can just about forgive anything except the way that another person made them feel."*

I am convinced that the key to providing five-star guest service is to treat people with these six attitudes. Guest service is simply about meeting the needs of another person in a warm and friendly manner. In reality it has very little to do with policies, manuals, rules and regulations. Great guest service is simply caring about others.

> *The greatest qualities are those that are most useful to other persons.*
> *– Aristotle*

The intelligent Golf Clubs always remember that every business transaction is about people helping other people meet a need. Our guests are really not asking for much. They simply would like to be served in a friendly and helpful manner. This will happen when we begin to understand that it must start with the right attitude...six to be exact.

Attitude #1

The Attitude of Friendliness

Guests first and foremost measure our service by the friendliness shown.

What word in the American language is more attractive than friendliness? The word itself makes us want to come closer. Ever since we have taken our first steps as a small child we have been attracted to those who are kind to us. This is one attitude that wins every time. People from all walks of life and every corner of the world appreciate when someone is nice to them.

I call this allure *the friendly factor*. In regards to the business world, most guests typically expect average run-of-the-mill service. They do not anticipate much in the area of sincere friendliness. Maybe it's because of our fast paced world and the busyness of life that make us forget to slow down just long enough to show someone some kindness.

When we are on the other side of the counter and play the role of a guest, we also expect the service to be somewhat average. *But when we encounter a person who is sincerely friendly to us we automatically feel that the service is wonderful!* This is because genuine friendliness is seldom expected in the marketplace. This little attitude will also give our guests a reason to tell others about the great service that we provide.

Why is friendliness so appealing? I believe that every human being is attracted to people who are kindhearted. Think of those in the past who were friendly to us for no apparent reason. In these memorable situations we may silently wonder why this person was so kind. In some cases we may even question the motive and secretly speculate if they are after something. The reason that we may be unsure about someone showing us kindness is because it usually happens so infrequently in our daily lives. But when we encounter someone who is genuinely friendly to us, there is something deep inside that wants to welcome it with open arms. Even though we may be uncertain at first to another's genuine kindness, in the end we all respond positively to these memorable moments.

As those who serve guests, we have the perfect occasion to show goodwill to others. It gives us a great opportunity to be friendly. *I believe this attitude alone can change an entire Golf Club if people simply understood the powerful attraction that kindness brings.* If an individual were to focus on being friendlier to others, he or she would instantly notice others going out of their way to be kind in return.

I am always puzzled when hearing stories about Golf Clubs that lack in the area of friendliness. The first thought that comes to mind is why any Golf Club would put staff members out in front who project an unfriendly attitude toward others. This not only makes guests feel uncomfortable, but also gives them a legitimate reason not to return in the future. I have witnessed this countless times in playing the role of a guest at different organizations. It made me want to depart as soon as possible. This of course is not a good thing for business.

Wherever there is a human being, there is an opportunity for kindness.
–Seneca

On the other hand I have had situations where a service representative has treated me with such consideration that I left feeling impressed by the kindness shown. *This left an indelible impression that the service was outstanding.* When I look back at those pleasant experiences I can now see that it was nothing more than one person showing kindness to another person. *The perception that I had of the service provided was enhanced simply because someone showed some unexpected friendliness.*

I am convinced that if more guest service representatives projected a little more consideration to each guest, the guest would walk away feeling that the service was outstanding. Why do I say this? Because guests as a whole do not expect it! I believe that guests always appreciate when unanticipated kindness is shown to them. This truth is universal. *In every business transaction, whether it is selling a product*

22

or providing a service, the guest is judging our service on the basis of whether or not we are serving them with an attitude of friendliness.

Let's look at an example of how friendliness plays a key role in projecting a first impression for the guest. Think about the restaurant business. The first contact made when stepping through the door is a greeting by someone who will seat us. This person will play a major role in how we feel about the restaurant. If the greeter is inattentive and hurried we may make a poor judgment about the overall service of the restaurant. If the greeter starts with a warm welcome and friendly smile, we automatically feel that the experience will be pleasant.

How can we be friendlier?

Don't wait for people to be friendly. Show them how.

I hope by now we can see how the attitude of friendliness plays a major role in how guests perceive our overall operation. But just knowing that this attitude is important in guest service is not enough. We can become convinced that showing kindness to our guests is essential in building a great service team, but still fail if we do not actually project it in our daily contact with guests. The goal is to learn some important guidelines that will help us become more considerate.

Having wisdom is knowing what to do next.
Having virtue is actually doing it.

The first guiding principle in providing great service is to realize that our job is to simply meet the requests of the guest. We are given the job of taking care of whatever need the guest may have at the moment. Since this is the first commandment of guest service, it seems only logical that we would want the service to be as pleasant as possible. If we understand that our job is to meet the guest's needs, our attitude should be as friendly as possible in order to make the overall experience wonderful.

The second guiding principle in learning to be friendlier is to ask ourselves how we like to be treated when we take on the role as a guest. I am convinced that 100% of us would declare that we would want to be treated in a friendly manner. This alone should convince us of the importance of how we should treat others. The age old saying that we should treat others in the manner that we would like to be treated is true in every facet of life, including serving our guests. And remember, Kindness, like a boomerang, always returns.

Kindness, like a boomerang, always returns.

Learning to be friendly takes practice. I once read a wise quote that said you learn to be kind by being kind. I would agree with this. Being friendly to others may come easy to some people, but that does not mean that everyone cannot improve in this department. The goal is to take small steps in showing kindness each day. Start off by greeting your guests with a smile and a more pleasant tone of voice. Learn to be more attentive and have the mindset that you are there for them. Others will quickly take notice of these little gestures. Soon you will begin to treat more and more people with genuine friendliness without even noticing that you are doing it. They in turn will begin to treat you in a more pleasant manner simply as a token of their appreciation in response to your unexpected kindness.

Friendliness starts with a smile

"I've never seen a smiling face that was not beautiful." - Unknown

In my first book, *Service Starts with a Smile*, I wrote about sixty-nine reasons why guests return. One of the incentives that draw people back is by making our environment more welcoming. The key is to create a friendly first impression. This can be accomplished simply by offering a pleasant smile to each guest. Without saying a word, this gesture will speak volumes and give a favorable impression to everyone who comes through our door.

Don't open a shop unless you like to smile.
- Chinese Proverb

The simple smile uses less facial muscles to produce and will create a warm and welcoming atmosphere. Here are five tips to assist in giving away more hospitable smiles:

Tip #1 Smiling takes practice

Smile - sunshine is good for your teeth.

In order to become more natural at smiling we need to practice. I know that this sounds odd but somewhere in our growing up years we have forgotten how to smile. Watch an infant and you will notice that most will freely give away smiles. Maybe this is one of the reasons they are so cute. Being able to smile takes a conscious effort for most adults. We somehow have lost this natural ability and would benefit greatly if we simply learned to smile more often. Not only will our looks instantaneously improve, but others will also feel more comfortable around us. *A smile is an inexpensive way to change our looks!* Someone once said that a smile confuses an approaching frown. When we offer a friendly smile, we are in essence showing kindness and creating a welcoming atmosphere for those who we come in contact with. So remember to practice and soon you will notice others smiling back at you.

Tip #2 what are you meditating on?

"Finally, brethren, whatsoever things are true, whatsoever things are honest, whatsoever things are just, whatsoever things are pure, whatsoever things are lovely, whatsoever things are of good report; if there be any virtue, and if there be any praise, think on these things." - Philippians 4:8

I have found that what we meditate on can have a major effect on how much smiling we do on a daily basis. Nothing can evaporate a smile more than keeping our mind on things that bring worry into our life.

"Don't tell me that worry doesn't do any good. I know better. The things I worry about never happen." - Unknown

Maybe that is why children can so easily smile. Their minds are not cluttered with a collection of files that remind us to fret. *I believe worrying has to go down as the number one way to waste time.* It has never accomplished anything positive. Maybe it's time to change your thinking if you have lost the natural ability to smile. Starting today begin to think of things that are virtuous. Get into the habit of meditating on right and excellent thoughts. Before long you will find yourself smiling more often. People will soon take notice and return a smile back!

Tip #3 Get rid of the "I Disease"

The measure of friendliness that people show is a reflection of the way we have treated them.

Another sure way to smile less is getting too focused on ourselves. This is called the "I Disease" where life revolves around me, myself and I. Not only is this detrimental to providing great guest service, but it will also quickly wipe away a friendly smile in no time. *I have found that people who smile easily are unselfish and genuinely show a concern for others.* On the other hand, those who simply live for themselves rarely smile because of the emptiness that selfishness brings. Life is so much more than exclusively trying to meet our own wants and needs. If we truly want to smile more we need to discover that it is only in giving of ourselves in serving others that we find fulfillment. Learn to be more interested in helping others and you will soon find yourself smiling more.

Tip #4 Learn to laugh again

A laugh is a smile that bursts.

Laughter truly is like medicine in that it not only will improve our health but also will assist us in learning to smile more. I believe that everyone would benefit if they just took time to laugh. Watch a group of children and we will hear laughter fill the air. Maybe it's the responsibilities of adult life that closes the door to spontaneous laughter in later years. Whatever the reason, we need to laugh more. Some people have described laughter as a great way to take an internal bath. I agree. People who laugh easily are usually the ones who freely give away smiles. *These people also attract others simply because of their carefree nature.* If we want to smile more it may also be worth our effort to replace any lingering worries with wholesome laughter. Our guests will gladly welcome and appreciate it.

Tip #5 Each day is a gift

Today is a gift; that is why they call it "the present."

Sometimes it can be the elementary reminders that awaken us to the things that really matter. *We need to be reminded that every day of life is truly a gift.* It is important to appreciate this gift if we are to smile more. We have all heard that life is too short to squander away. Each person is allowed 24 hours a day and is given a choice in how he or she will use it. When we look at life as a moment-by-moment gift that should be enjoyed, we will learn to express this appreciation with a friendlier countenance. This alone should give us all the more reason to smile.

Being friendly toward others is one of the most difficult things to give away - it is usually returned.

Attitude #2
The Attitude of Enthusiasm
Serving with enthusiasm adds to the guest's overall experience.

Have you ever met someone who was enthused about something? It could be about anything. More than likely you were drawn in by their zeal. Now imagine coming across someone who was enthused about life. Everything they did was done with interest and excitement. How would that make you feel? More than likely you would be attracted to their passion for living. *The reason for our attraction is that when we are confronted with a person full of enthusiasm, it somehow awakens something inside of us.* We feel something that may have been dormant for years. This is exactly what enthusiasm does to others. It drives them to search into their own lives and wonder whatever happened to the excitement that past dreams and memories once brought.

The attitude of enthusiasm is an invisible force that is felt immediately by others. When we are excited to serve, we will not only excel as guest service representatives but will have people talking about our service. Consider the times you have been served exceptionally and you will find that the person did it with enthusiasm. I have personally witnessed guest service superstars who were so passionate about their product or service that they could not help but serve with enthusiasm. They simply gave their best.

I am convinced that without enthusiasm guest service becomes more of a duty to perform. When we are not excited about serving others, we somehow begin to lose our balance in providing our guests with excellent service. On the other hand, when we truly enjoy what we do it will show in the way we perform. No other attitude can make us more passionate about our duties. Being enthused makes others take notice and will consistently deliver better service to our guests. *They walk away and feel that the service was outstanding simply because of our eagerness to serve them.*

Let me share an example of how enthusiasm can decide on the overall experience when serving guests. Recently one evening I took my family for ice cream after church. The ice cream parlor we decided on was more upscale than your typical parlor. In the past we have visited this store and were pleased with the service. When we walked in we were greeted with loud music that would appeal to a very small segment of society (who more than likely would not patronize this place.) The two young girls working behind the counter immediately gave the impression by their faces that this was the last place they wanted to be. There would be no friendly greeting or smiles. As we were ready to order our ice cream, one of the girls blurted out something to the effect of "please fire me." It was a very odd comment to announce to a guest. They were definitely not thrilled to be there.

After leaving I thought about our experience. We were excited to get some ice cream with the kids but were immediately turned off by the lack of enthusiasm displayed by the servers. I also thought about how much the owner must be paying for rent at this upscale outdoor mall, and if he realized that these two employees were driving guests away. I believe that someone somewhere had made a severe miscalculation in hiring these two employees. They did not understand basic 101 guest service.

If I had owned this ice cream parlor, I would hire employees who showed the most enthusiasm. I would want people who were excited to scoop up ice cream. Here is the reason why. Everyone who goes out for ice cream is thrilled about the prospects of tasting their favorite flavor. If this ice cream parlor had simply hired employees who projected the same excitement about serving the ice cream, the whole experience for the guest would be greatly enhanced. Guests would walk away with the feeling that the ice cream is the best around. This not only goes for ice cream parlors, but can also apply to restaurants, theme parks, roller rinks, clothing stores, resorts, insurance companies, clubs, and a thousand other businesses. *What we need to understand is that guests on the most part will consider our service dazzling if we simply understand that serving them with enthusiasm would enhance their overall experience.*

Imagine that you and your family decided to go out to your favorite restaurant. When you enter the doors you are greeted in a welcoming manner and seated. A few minutes later a friendly and enthused waitress appears to serve you and your family. All of a sudden the whole experience of going out for dinner is enhanced simply because the people were excited to serve your family. We could easily replace going to a restaurant with getting a haircut. You walk into the store and are greeted kindly with a warm smile and told that it will be five minutes. A few minutes pass and your name is called out by a friendly voice. The hair stylist seems genuinely interested about being able to cut your hair. She then asks about your preferences and you sense that she is really listening as you describe how you would like to look ten years younger. She responds by telling you that she is a beautician, not a magician. She then laughs and continues to be enthused about having the honor of cutting your hair. She somehow gives you the impression that you are a VIP guest. After leaving a hefty tip, you walk away feeling that the service was outstanding.

When guests decide to make a purchase on a product or service, they are usually excited about the prospects of acquiring it. *We as guest service representatives need to realize that our enthusiasm will increase their enthusiasm as well. When we are excited for them, they in turn become more excited about the purchase.* This is important to understand. I am convinced that most bad experiences that guests remember at Golf Clubs are largely due to being served by a staff member who shows no enthusiasm for serving. On the other hand, great experiences are a result of being served by those who are excited about the prospects of serving their guests.

How Can We Be More Enthused?

Having enthusiasm is simply a by-product of having an appreciation for life.

Hopefully we have made the point that enthusiasm can greatly enhance the overall experience for the guest. But how do we become more enthused about the prospects of serving others? What will inspire and motivate us to see serving as a privilege? If having enthusiasm has so many positive benefits, then why doesn't everyone develop more excitement into their lives? These are great questions. *My first thought is that enthusiasm must come from a sincere appreciation for life. When we see life as a gift not to be wasted, our whole outlook will be positively changed.* We will begin to see that each day is to be lived with passion and zeal. This new appreciation that life is a gift will not only enhance our daily lives but also carry over in serving others with enjoyment and passion.

I have always been fascinated by the true stories of those who were in dire straits and somehow survived a life and death situation. I have read accounts of those who survived after floating on a raft in the middle of the ocean for over thirty days with no food. Other true stories that have continually grabbed my attention describe men and women who survived being lost or trapped in uninhabited locations for days on end with little hope of survival. I have also read accounts of those who survived prisoner of war camps and somehow made it through to find freedom once again. Without exception, every one of these brave people who survived such grim circumstances had one commonality: *They all appreciated the simple gift of life after being rescued. We find that these people developed a new enthusiasm and appreciation for simply being alive.*

Maybe you know of someone who has survived a near fatal auto accident or a sickness that had threatened their life. Maybe that someone was you. Whatever the case may be, *people in these situations tend to come out with a deeper appreciation for life.* I believe this occurs because getting through a life-threatening experience makes these survivors appreciate that they are given a second chance at life. These survivors wake up each morning and recognize that life is precious and not to be taken for granted. *They have a new belief that every day is a gift.*

I bring up these moving survivor stories to say that we can live with enthusiasm if we see life as a gift. I would like to think that every person has the ability to recapture this enthusiasm for life without having to survive on a raft for thirty days in the middle of a shark infested ocean. *Having enthusiasm is simply a by-product of having an appreciation for life.* We do not need to go through dire straits to appreciate that life is to be lived with enjoyment. Those who are grateful for the gift of life show it by their passion. I believe that this is the key if we are to serve others with more enthusiasm.

Six Benefits of Enthusiasm

None are as old as those who have outlived enthusiasm.

Being an enthusiastic person on and off the job adds so much more to our lives. As mentioned earlier, *enthusiasm attracts simply because it awakens something in others.* This attitude allures others because they see how much we enjoy life. Enthusiastic people have an appreciation for life that draws others in. Being enthused to serve will only add to the overall experience for the guest. They in turn appreciate the fact that we have served them with enjoyment. Guests will give our service a higher rating because of this attitude. They in turn will walk away with a bit of enthusiasm themselves simply because of our zest for serving them. Let's look at six additional benefits that an attitude of enthusiasm will bring into our lives.

1. Enthusiastic people turn no's into yes's

Just say no to negativism. - Bumper Sticker

This benefit is huge when it comes to guest service. Enthusiastic people tend to say yes much more than they say no. *When we are excited about serving others, we will have a tendency to say yes more often to our guests.* On the other hand, I have seen unenthused guest service representatives who acted as though they were excited to say no to their guests. Being a person who can turn no's into yes's will not only draw guests back, but also make the overall experience more enjoyable. Enthusiastic people tend to give better service and will find any way possible to meet whatever need there is. This attitude makes the service provided a more positive experience because of the optimistic outlook that enthusiasm communicates to others.

2. Enthusiastic people tend to be happier

Success on the job can be measured by the amount of enthusiasm we had in our career.

I truly believe that happy employees make happy guests. When we are happy on the job, our guests will take notice by the excellent service that we provide for them. This is why having an attitude of enthusiasm is so important on the job. *Think of the times that you have felt happy in life. More than likely being enthusiastic about something caused it.* Maybe we captured our enthusiasm simply in recognizing that life itself is a gift to be treasured. Whatever the reason, one of the triggers that made us happy was having an attitude of enthusiasm. They really do go hand-in-hand. We will always perform at our best when we enjoy our profession. Being enthused about serving is no different. When we enjoy our work we will show it by our enthusiasm and satisfaction. These two traits will be recognized by the excellent service we provide to our guests.

3. Enthusiastic people see solutions

Any great movement in the pages of history has been the result of enthusiasm.

Another great benefit of having an attitude of enthusiasm is that it tends to help us see solutions more clearly. This inner attitude allows us to focus more on finding solutions and less on clinging to problems. Enthusiasm gives us the motivation needed to seek answers. We become better at problem solving. Setbacks are looked at as challenges. This will only make us better at serving our guests because of the various roadblocks that can arise during a course of a day. Our focus on seeking solutions also gives us a more positive outlook in life. We stop dwelling on problems and begin seeking solutions. This has a big impact on how well we deliver service to our guests. They will sense that we are doing our best to serve them because of our positive outlook at meeting their needs.

4. Enthusiastic people show appreciation

Enthusiasm allows us to appreciate life more.

The fourth benefit that enthusiastic people have is how easily they can convey to the guest their appreciation. Guests will always be thankful when we show how much we appreciate them patronizing our Golf Club. There is something to be said about giving others the sense that they are appreciated. *If we as guest service representatives could grasp how powerful expressing gratitude is to our guests, we would take every opportunity to show more appreciation.* I am convinced that letting our guests know how much we value them will bring them back time and again. I also believe that the people who are most qualified to express appreciation to others are those who have an attitude of enthusiasm. Think of the times that someone showed you appreciation. More than likely you remembered it simply because of their excitement and sincere gratitude. As guest service representatives, our guests will remember our sincere appreciation if we express it with sincere enthusiasm. *Without this, the expression of gratitude tends to lack authenticity.*

5. Enthusiastic people send a message

Genius is nothing more than inflamed enthusiasm.

When we are enthused about the product or service we are selling, our attitude will send a message to the guest. This is important because of the feeling of self-assurance that it will give to those who are served by us. *The message that we express with our enthusiastic attitude conveys that we are confident that the product or service will meet the guest's immediate needs.*

As an example, if we were in the restaurant business and hired servers who believed that the food tasted excellent, we would want to make sure that they positively expressed this to every guest who entered our doors. The best way to do this would be to have employees who knew how to communicate enthusiasm when being asked about a certain item on the menu. If we express with excitement that the chicken potpie is the best in town *(and we truly believe it)*, our way of expressing this to our guests would assure them that it would be a great choice. This is why it is so important to hire people who are enthused about the product or service that we are presenting to the guest. This attitude alone sends a secure feeling to our guests and will give them the self assurance that they have made the right choice.

6. Enthusiastic people make things happen

Some of the world's greatest feats were accomplished by people not smart enough to know they were impossible.

The final benefit in having an enthusiastic attitude is that it allows us to make things happen. By this I mean that enthusiasm has a way of motivating us to get things done in an efficient manner. Because of our positive outlook, we are better equipped to meet the guest's immediate needs in a timely fashion. *Without enthusiasm, we would be less motivated and willing to give our guests the best service possible.* Having this attitude jumpstarts our motivation to take care of others.

On the other hand, being unmotivated is essentially a sign that a person lacks enthusiasm. This deficiency can be detrimental if our job is to serve others. Being enthused will give us a big advantage in that it will inspire us to deliver outstanding service. *I have found that every guest service superstar that I have encountered can make things happen simply because he or she was motivated to make my experience as pleasurable as possible.* This never would have been the case if they had lacked the enthusiasm to serve. In the final analysis, people with enthusiasm will always be the best qualified to make things happen in order to provide the best possible service to their guests.

Success is going from failure to failure without a loss of enthusiasm. -
Winston Churchill

Attitude #3

The Attitude of Caring
Loyalty occurs when guests sense that we genuinely care.

Of all attitudes in existence, none is more powerful than the attitude of caring about others. This attitude alone will determine the outcome of every relationship in life. It far outweighs any other attitude simply because it is the cornerstone by which every other attitude will manifest itself. No other attitude will determine our fate quite like how much we care for others. In essence, caring will be the attitude that will ultimately measure the qualities of our relationships both on and off the job.

When we truly have a heart that cares for others, our life will begin to take on more meaning. Guests will also quickly take notice of our sincere desire to serve them when we genuinely care that their visit was enjoyable. Loyalty also begins to happen when our guests sense that meeting their needs is more important than simply making a sale. We feel reassured when we sense that another person cares about us. It provides for us a feeling of security and support. It also reinforces our

36

connection with others. *Caring is one of the best things we can do for our health.*

As mentioned earlier, this attitude will have a major influence on every other attitude that has taken a hold of us. When we care about others, we will find that our disposition will be friendlier. We will be more respectful and tend to encourage others more frequently. Guests will also be more attracted to us because they will sense that we truly are looking out for them. Without having to say anything, they will quickly sense by our actions that we can be trusted and will do whatever it takes to make their experience at our Golf Club as enjoyable as possible. On the other hand, guests will sense when we do not care about meeting their needs. Whether we care or not will be projected in various ways to them. This attitude is difficult to hide because of the many signs that eventually come out. Let's look at three basic clues that will allow our guests to sense whether or not we are truly looking out for their best interests.

The face cannot hide

The first noticeable clue that guests will always measure when they are about to be served is a quick read of the face. Whether we realize it or not, each one of us eventually becomes proficient at reading others simply by doing an inventory of their facial expressions. A quick glance can indicate whether or not the person is interested in serving us. One of the first areas that we look at is the person's eyes. They say that the eyes are the windows to the soul. Studying a person's eyes can tell us a lot about whether or not the person is interested in helping us or simply performing a duty.

As guest service representatives, it's important to let both our eyes and smiles come through loud and clear. *Friendly eyes matched with a friendly smile will not only tell our guests that we are happy to see them, but will also convey that we genuinely care.* That is one major reason that a friendly smile can go a long way in expressing that we genuinely care about meeting their needs.

The tone of our voice

Don't look at me in that tone of voice!

It's been said that the tone of our voice accounts for approximately 38% of what the listener gets from the message, 55% from our body language, and only 7% from what is actually being said. *As humans, we quickly adapt our listening more to the tone of what is being said and less on what actually is said.* Our guests will measure us in the same manner. It is important to allow our tone of voice to speak in such a way as to convey to our guests that we care about meeting their needs. One simple way to do this is by learning to talk to our guests and not at them. A friendly tone of voice will express that we care. Learning to speak clearly and in a gracious manner will give others the impression that we are there for them.

Actions speak louder than words

He that does good to another does good also to himself. -Seneca

We have all heard the expression that actions speak louder than words. When everything is said and done, the measurement of whether or not we care about our guests will always be revealed by our actions. Words are just words until we put some shoe leather to them. Our first priority as service representatives is to take care of our guest's immediate needs. The way to do this to make sure our words match our actions. If we make a promise it is paramount that we follow up with an action to that promise. When we show this through consistent follow up action, our guests will eventually develop loyalty because of the trust that we have earned from them. Our actions express to them that we truly do care.

Developing an Attitude of Caring

Caring about others provides us with the key for unlocking better relationships and making them more genuine.

Because caring has a major influence on every other attitude that we carry with us, it is important that we take an inventory of how much care we project to our guests. *I am convinced that every other attitude will be changed for the better when we learn to care more about others, including the guests who visit our Golf Club.* In order to develop a more caring attitude, the first step that must occur is to take a personal inventory of how much we truly care. I know this seems like an odd thing to ask, but how can we improve in this area unless we take an honest look and measure if there is any room for improvement. Do we project to our guests *(and others for that matter)* that we genuinely care that their experience at our Golf Club is enjoyable, or do they sense that we are just there to earn a paycheck? There is a big difference in these two attitudes, and both will be reflected in how well we serve. Guests will be able to tell in no time how much care we put into our service.

Once we have taken a closer, more personal look at our own measure of caring, we then will want to consider ways to improve on developing genuine concern for the needs of others. As mentioned, I am convinced that this attitude alone would begin to transform any Golf Club. Guests will sense this and begin to tell others about their wonderful experience. If we are to look at improving this attitude, it may help to discover what caring actually looks like in real life. *I have found four traits that have been evident in every person that I have found who consistently portrays a caring attitude.* Let's look at these four characteristics and see if they can help us to discover how we can become better at caring for others.

Four Traits commonly found in a caring attitude

The more we care for the welfare of others, the more we will begin to notice how others care for us. We begin to find that what goes around eventually comes around.

#1 Patience reflects a caring attitude

"How far you go in life depends on your being tender with the young, compassionate with the aged, sympathetic with the striving and tolerant of the weak and strong. Because someday in life you will have been all of these." - George Washington Carver

One of the first traits that I have consistently found in people with a caring attitude is their ability to be patient. Not only will this attract others, but will also become a major advantage for those who display patience when serving others. As guest service representatives, having patience will always make our guests feel more comfortable. The reason for this is because when we display a sense of calmness for every type of situation that is bound to occur, our guests are given comfort in knowing we will be able to meet their needs in a professional and efficient manner. This is due to the fact that patient people tend to be calmer in various situations.

Being a patient person is a quality that is esteemed throughout the world. Every society considers this trait to be highly valued. *The reason for this is that it conveys a sense of self-control in the one who consistently shows to be patient with others.* Whenever I sense that I am being served by a patient person, my sense of importance is suddenly enhanced. I feel that this person is giving me the right to express my immediate needs as a guest without feeling that I am intruding on his or her time. *Patient people also have a way of making us feel accepted simply by their calm disposition. This of course creates an atmosphere that is warm and welcoming.*

Being patient with others may come easy to those who tend to have the genetic make-up of being more understanding. But this does not mean that we cannot all learn to be a little more patient with others. I have discovered that times of testing our character are great proving grounds for developing more patience. Whenever we may go through a difficult situation in our own lives, it can become the perfect climate for exercising more patience. I have found that those who tend to be more patient with people have personally experienced difficulties in the past that eventually made them more understanding toward others. I believe these times of trials can also help to develop more character if we will only learn from them.

Patience is the companion of wisdom. - St. Augustine

#2 Listening reflects a caring attitude

Much silence makes a powerful noise.

When I first met my wife Carol at college, I was immediately impressed with her ability to listen. As I babbled away I could not help but notice how she continued to pay attention to what I had to say. Over the years I have watched how my wife has attentively listened to other people. She truly is gifted with the "art of listening."

When we listen to others we are conveying to them that we care about what they have to say. We also are acknowledging their worth simply because we are giving them our undivided attention and allowing them to speak with no interruptions. This alone can have a powerful effect on others because it allows them to convey what they are thinking and gives the person a sense of importance. Another great benefit of listening is that it will always express consideration for others. To listen intently truly is one of the finest gifts that we can give to another person.

Listening is an attitude of the heart, a genuine desire to be with another that both attracts and heals.

Now imagine how our guests feel when we intently listen to what they have to say. When we give our full attention it conveys to them that we care about their needs. This automatically gives our guests a sense that we are there for them and want their experience at the Golf Club to be as enjoyable as possible. Guests will also rate our service more positive simply because we have taken the time to listen to what they have to say. They will walk away feeling validated and understood because of the consideration that we have communicated to them through the simple act of listening.

A good listener is not only popular everywhere, but after a while he or she knows something.

I am convinced that this gift can transform and help to develop healthier relationships. People will begin to be more honest with us because they will sense that we care about them. *Very rarely have I met someone who gave me the impression that they cared who did not listen well. It is as if caring and listening consistently go hand- in-hand.* I have always thought that if someone put an advertisement in the paper that simply stated they would do nothing but listen for a full hour, people would flock to them for the opportunity to express their thoughts without being interrupted.

It is the province of knowledge to speak and the privilege of wisdom to listen.

When we serve guests, it gives us the perfect opportunity to listen more and speak less. This is because we are there to meet their needs. But if we do not listen, it will be difficult to understand what their needs are. Listening allows us to give our guests the sense that we really care enough to want to give them what they would like, and not what we think they should have. We are showing them by our attentiveness that we care about them. This alone creates a wonderful experience for those we serve. Our listening allows them an opportunity to express their needs.

Asking questions shows our desire to listen

One of the greatest compliments we can give to a person is to ask their opinion and then listen closely to what they have to say.

When we do not listen to our guests we convey that we are not interested in meeting their needs. This can be detrimental to any business. Let's use an example. If I sold a certain product I would ask questions and find out exactly what the guest is looking for. *This would tell them right away that I am more interested in what they want and less on what I would like to sell them.* Being able to ask questions is a wonderful way to show others that we are listeners. Being able to ask the right questions is a gift that allows guests to open up. If we are to consistently deliver outstanding service, our goal must be to meet and exceed our guest's expectations. The only way we will be able to do this is to make inquires that will then allow the guest to openly share. This also will give the feeling that we are there for them.

"The greatest gift we can give another is our undivided attention."

The interest that is conveyed by our questions will then give each guest a positive reason to speak highly of our service. It is the combination of asking the right questions and listening intently that will win our guests.

#3 Acceptance reflects a caring attitude

When people are asked to remember a person who meant a lot to them in life, they usually remember someone who really cared and understood them.

Another telling sign of a caring attitude is being able to accept others unconditionally. Having this characteristic in our personality is powerful in attracting guests. The reason for this is that we all appreciate when others show us acceptance. It is as if we have an inner need to be received by others. When we have a caring attitude, others will soon take notice of the way we show acceptance toward them. This is essential if we are to attract guests because of the wide range of people that we will be serving on a daily basis. When we express to others a sense of acceptance, they in turn feel more comfortable and will want to come back in the future.

One of the most important goals of any Golf Club is to create an environment for the guest that is friendly and welcoming. This can only occur when we communicate unconditional acceptance toward those who walk through our doors. Consistently giving this sense of welcoming to guests will have a positive influence on their decision to return. Over the years I have had experiences as a guest that has made me realize the importance of feeling accepted. There have been memories with a variety of Golf Clubs that have been both pleasant and not so pleasant. *As I recall these experiences, I am always amazed to see how the level of acceptance I felt determined my overall rating for the service that was provided.* The Golf Clubs that I felt provided excellent service had a way of making their guests feel welcomed and accepted.

Providing our guests a sense of acceptance will go a long way in making them feel more welcomed at our club. In the mind of the guest, if the service starts off with a friendly welcome, they will give our service a higher rating. *This is why it will make all the difference if we simply give each guest a warm and friendly welcome.* This alone is the key in providing them with a sense of acceptance. Not only will we show that we care but also offer them a great reason to want to return.

#4 Being nice reflects a caring attitude

Genuine kindness is doing something nice for someone who will never find out.

A final characteristic of a caring attitude is that it will show itself through kindheartedness. Caring people tend to always be kind and friendly toward others. *I have never met someone who I considered to be caring who did not also show kindness toward others.* This caring attitude has consistently showed itself through benevolence. Reflect on the times of meeting someone who you considered to be friendly. More than likely you enjoyed their presence because of the way they made you feel. *If we look deeper, we will find that they were liked because of a kind attitude toward us. This caring is what true relationships are built upon.*

Earlier I focused on the attitude of friendliness and how influential it is in providing outstanding guest service. The reason for this is because when we show ourselves to be friendly toward others, we are sending a message of acceptance. *We are also meeting a basic need of giving them a sense of belonging. Kindness has a way of doing this.* Without kindness, our guests will sense that they are not welcomed and will look for the nearest exit door.

Guests who may consider doing business are measuring us by how accepted we make them feel. The intelligent service teams understand this and focus on creating a friendly atmosphere by hiring those who have what I had earlier coined *the friendly factor.* These are people who tend to have a disposition that consistently shows consideration toward others. When Golf Clubs understand this and hire friendly people to meet and greet the guest, there will be a sudden change in how each guest perceives the service provided. *Guests who encounter these Golf Clubs that hire based on the friendly factor will desire to come back simply because of the acceptance felt every time they enter the doors.*

On the other hand, when a Golf Club does not take into account the power of friendliness, they can miss out in hiring the right people for the job. I have often thought that hiring people who will be working with the public should first and foremost be based on being able to communicate in a kind and friendly manner. Of course this can be difficult because of the problem of how to measure kindness. But if the hiring team can learn to ask the right questions, they may be able to hire the candidates who have the friendly factor. *Hiring the right people can make or break the guest's perception of the service being provided.*

The power of caring

Men are only as great as they are kind.

I hope by now we recognize how influential a caring attitude is on every Golf Club that provides guest service. As mentioned earlier, caring about others is the foundation by which every other attitude grows out from. When we care about others our life will reflect such character traits as being kind to others, showing respect, and appreciating what people do for us. Let's look at a list of nine esteemed qualities that will shine forth when we genuinely have a caring heart.

#1 We will be patient toward others

As discussed earlier, patience is one of the qualities that a caring attitude will consistently bring forth. Not only will our guests quickly take notice when we serve them with a heart of patience, but they will be more receptive toward us.

#2 We will listen more

The first duty of caring is to listen.

As mentioned earlier, the more we listen, the more it will show that we care. When we give the gift of listening to our guests, they in turn will consistently give our service a higher rating. Listening does two important things for our guests. First it conveys our concern about meeting their needs. Second, and more importantly, it validates that we care.

#3 We will be less selfish

No man is more cheated than the selfish man.

Another valued characteristic that a caring attitude will bring forth is selflessness. This is because caring makes us focus more on others and less on ourselves. This is one of the beautiful features of capturing an attitude that cares for others. Whether we realize it or not, guests will notice when we are more focused on ourselves because of the attitude that selfishness tends to bring forth. This "all about me" attitude also makes it difficult to provide exceptional service simply because of an unwillingness to take our eyes off of ourselves. But when we begin to focus on others and their needs, our entire life begins to become more fulfilling.

#4 We will be more understanding

The capacity to care is the thing which gives our life its deepest significance.

When we have an attitude of caring it will also make us more understanding toward others. *We will begin to be more thoughtful with our words and actions.* Understanding simply means that we begin to sense what others may be feeling. As guest service representatives, having this sensitivity will help us to understand how guests would like to be treated. We will begin to recognize actions in our own conduct that may be detrimental in being able to deliver excellent service. *We also will begin to ask ourselves if we are treating others the way that we would like to be treated.* By learning to be more understanding, our attitude will begin to change and make a big difference in how we deliver service toward others.

#5 We will show more concern

In about the same degree as you are helpful, you will be happy.

An attitude of caring will show itself in our concern for others. People will sense that we are concerned about their welfare because of the way we treat them. When we show concern, it allows our guests to trust us and feel more comfortable in our presence. But if our actions do not reflect that we care, our guests will be less likely to tell others about us because of the lack of trust. As a result, our Golf Club will suffer because guests will eventually find a place where they feel others can be trusted by the genuine concern that is shown.

#6 We will be more confident

People who think about others will also be more confident simply because a caring heart reflects inner security. *The act of caring about others takes a measure of security. When we are weighted down with inner insecurities, it becomes much harder to genuinely care.* The reason for this is that when we are insecure, it becomes more difficult to open up and meet the needs of others. Having a caring attitude can be said to be a reflection of inner confidence.

#7 We will have more empathy

Being empathetic is the basis of morality.

Being empathetic toward others is a sign that we have an attitude of caring. *Empathetic people have the ability to step inside another person and feel what he or she may be experiencing at any given moment.* One of the main reasons that this attitude is considered a quality is because it allows us to be more accepting and less judgmental toward others. We learn to give people the benefit of the doubt and in turn become more considerate for what others may be going through.

#8 We will be more sharing

People who genuinely care for others show it by their willingness to share. By this I mean that they are more willing to give of themselves more often. Like selflessness, having the gift of sharing allows us to focus our attention on meeting the needs of others. We become more others-focused and less me-focused. The saying that states "sharing is caring" holds true. In the end, it is only when we have a heart of caring that will allow us to gladly share and serve others with no reservations.

#9 We will be more sincere

Guests will be able to tell the difference between required courtesy and sincere care.

The final quality that a caring attitude will project to others is a sincerity to serve them. I find this to be one of the most important qualities that caring people have in common. *To be sincere in our caring simply means that there are no strings attached. Our reasons for caring are not tainted with hidden agendas. We care with no ulterior motive.* Our heart is right because we genuinely care for the welfare of others. Guests cannot help but be attracted to this type of service because they will sense our sincere concern for them. Offering outstanding guest service can be summed up in the following thought:

In the final analysis, providing outstanding guest service will only work when we genuinely care about our guests.

Attitude #4

The Attitude of Respect

Giving respect shows our willingness to serve others.

There is one attitude that every person longs to receive from others. It does not matter if the person is eight or eighty. It makes no difference whether the person resides in a remote village in the middle of nowhere or makes his or her home in a major city. Each one of us is openly receptive when others express it to us. This attractive attitude that I am talking about is when we show others respect. There is no attitude quite as appealing as when we genuinely communicate our respect. It not only validates others, but also gives them a sense of dignity. *When we encounter a person who is respectful toward us, we tend to straighten up and present our best selves to them. This is the beauty and benefit of showing respect. It allows us to bring out the best in people.*

When we have self-respect, it becomes easy to give respect to others. I have found that there is no greater attitude for being our best both on and off the job than having self-respect. It is something that allows us to be all that we can be. As service representatives, when we show our guests respect, we are conveying to them that we have self-respect as well as a willingness to serve them. *This attitude also gives our guests a sense of honor and admiration because of the high regard that is communicated through respect.* It gives our guests a feeling that we admire and appreciate that they have decided to do business with us. This feeling should consistently be conveyed. Guests are important and without them our Golf Club would eventually close.

The mentality that every service representative should have is one where he or she views the guest as essential to the overall success of the club. When we look at guests as the ones who will assist in making our Golf Club successful, our attitude toward them will begin to change in a more positive manner. The key in winning loyalty starts with respect.

Do we just give respect to anyone?

Treat everyone with kindness, even those who may be rude to you – not because they are nice, but because you are.

Some will say that respect is something that must be earned. It's been said that unless a person has earned respect, we do not have to grant it to him or her. But is this really the way that it should be? Are we to show respect only to those who deserve it? We have all known people who tended to be deficient in the area of self-respect. They not only show little respect for themselves, but also rarely show it toward others. Is it then all right to withhold showing respect to those who appear to be without self-respect? What about those people *(including our guests)* who rarely show respect to us? Does this give us an excuse to treat them the way that they have treated us? These are tough questions, but let me share a thought that may help.

Let us say that we lived in a perfect world where everyone treated each other with dignity and respect. If this were the case, it would be easy to treat each person with the same kind of respect that we continually received. But of course this is not the case. We live in a world where every person can fall into a moment of not showing someone proper courtesy. This especially can be the case when our job is to serve guests. We never know what is coming next. The day may be going great when out of the clear blue we encounter a guest who may be having an off day. So what happens? Out of nowhere we have just been spoken to in an ill-mannered tone of voice. Caught by surprise, we take a deep breath in an attempt to compose ourselves for what may be ahead. Without warning, we may have just encountered a guest who could possibly be frustrated about something that is totally disconnected from us. Do we give it right back or is there a better way to handle this disrespectful attitude that has been shown to us?

We should be too big to take offense and too noble to give it.
- Abraham Lincoln

51

There is a better way

The way to find out if we truly have a servant's heart is examine our attitude when others actually treat us like a servant.

As long as we work with guests, we will encounter those who may be having a difficult day. For all we know, they may have just received a parking ticket or lost a dear friend. Whatever the case may be, there is a better way to handle disrespectful behavior toward us. And what is that way? *Show them respect!* I know what you may be thinking right now. In your mind you are saying that it is much easier to say than to do. *But giving our discontented guest a dose of respect will 99.9% of the time make them embarrassed that they have just treated us in such an ill-mannered way.*

It's important to understand that our goal is not to embarrass anyone or try to seek revenge in any way. *Our goal if we are to become guest service superstars is simply to help them out in the best possible way. Showing respect after being disrespected is the best way to handle impolite manners.* The reason for this is that it not only will calm the majority of guests, but will also help the guest to realize that their behavior was inappropriate. *We did not have to say a word.* Our actions in maintaining our own self-respect will show our unhappy guest that we also care about them even though they may have treated us in a disrespectful manner. In the end, it may even come about that our unhappy guest apologizes for their behavior and becomes our most valued guest in the future!

Self-respect brings a respectful attitude

Self-respect permeates all aspects of our life.

If respecting others is one of the highest qualities in human relationships, why is it so difficult for some to do? *I believe one main reason is because of a lack of self-respect. If we do not have respect for ourselves, how can we expect to give it to others?* In other words, how can we value another person if we do not value ourselves? When we respect ourselves it becomes much easier to express a healthy admiration toward others. Having self-dignity is the best platform for living with an attitude of respect. I believe the true superstars of guest service have this as their advantage. Not only do they maintain their own self-respect, but they also have no difficulty in showing others good old-fashioned courtesy.

How can we be more respectful?

By now I hope it has become clear that being able to respect others is an outcome of maintaining self-respect in our own lives. When we walk with integrity, we will have very little difficulty in showing others respect. As I have learned from those whom I regard as having an attitude of respect, I have observed eight qualities that reflect their lives. The following eight traits will assist us in building a more respectful attitude toward others.

Building a respectful attitude tip #1...
Have a high regard for others

I remember meeting a young man from the south that impressed me from the start by his well-behaved manners. This man had a great habit of showing respect to everyone he met. His mannerisms and demeanor toward others were outstanding. He simply had a way about himself that attracted others. *When I look back at this man's behavior, it becomes crystal-clear that he had a high regard for everyone that he met. His obvious politeness and tone of voice drew people in because of the way he honored them with his respectful attitude.*

Having a high regard for our guests will have the same effect if we understand that every guest deserves to be treated with dignity. Like the young man who showed courtesy to everyone he met, we too can learn to be this way toward others. Whether it is a guest coming in our doors or a neighbor down the street, being respectful will naturally happen more frequently if we learn to value each person as being important. Every person arrives into the world the same way. When we begin to see the true worth of individuals, we will improve on treating them with respect. Learning to have a high regard for others will transform our behavior into one of kindness, admiration, and respect.

Building a respectful attitude tip #2...
Learn to encourage others

Another great way to build a respectful attitude is to learn to encourage people. *If we are to be more honoring toward others it is paramount that we learn to support people with our words and actions.* In my own experiences I have found that those who have a consistent attitude of respect encourage others. They also attract guests by their positive way of giving a thoughtful word at the right time. Respectful people have a way of making others feel better because of their encouraging support. Very rarely will we find words of discouragement coming from a person who respects others. *They understand the power of words and choose them carefully.*

When we are with a person who has an attitude of respect, we are more inclined to be on our best behavior. *Respectful people also understand the strength that an encouraging word brings.* I believe that more words of affirmation would take place if we truly understood the power of words. Later in the chapter we will be discussing more on the topic of encouraging others. But for now, remember that a word of encouragement will go a long way in showing others respect.

Building a respectful attitude tip #3...
See the potential in others

See others not as they are, but what they can become.

If we want to build a more respectful attitude toward others, we need to see each person's potential. Showing others respect simply means that we value them as a person just like ourselves. We are no better or no worse. In my own life, I have had people who believed that I could improve or become something more. I cannot tell you how much I have respected them for seeing something that I did not recognize at the time. This is the beauty of showing others respect. *It allows people to pick themselves up and believe that they can move forward.* Our respectful attitude also gives a person a sense of dignity. When we see the potential in others, they in turn begin to stand taller. This is the positive power of respecting others.

Because life can be filled with peaks and valleys, it is important to keep in mind that we can never truly know where a person is at in his or her own life. This is why prejudices and critical attitudes are detrimental in building healthy relationships. Not only do these attitudes keep us from being respectful, but also a judgmental attitude makes others uncomfortable in our presence. As service representatives, our first duty is to create a warm and welcoming atmosphere for each guest. If we want to create an accepting environment, it is important to look through the eyes of grace and see the potential in others.

Building a respectful attitude tip #4...
Learn to be pliable

You can accomplish by kindness what you cannot by force.
- Publilius Syrus

Having an attitude of respect toward others means that we do not have to always have our own way. Learning to respect the opinion of others and not demanding our own way all of the time is a quality found in a respectful person. Being courteous means allowing others to make decisions without sulking. It's being pliable and allowing other people to make the choice. *When a person always has to have it his or her own way, others will feel disrespected because their opinion was not considered.* It would be like a few friends going out for pizza and the same person always insisting on mushrooms without considering that the others may not care for them. What this conveys is a sign of disrespect because their opinions were not regarded. If we always insist on our own way, we will soon find very few people wanting to join us for pizza.

Learning to be pliable on the job is critical if we are to get along with our fellow staff members. When we continually demand that things be done our way, we are expressing that we do not care about what others may think. In leadership this can be deadly for building a great guest service staff. Excellent managers are flexible and allow co-workers to openly share ideas on how to improve the overall operation. *Being pliable is a great way to show that we truly respect the opinion of others.*

Building a respectful attitude tip #5...
Respect yourself first

The first building block in being respectful toward others is having self-respect. When we live by such qualities as honesty and integrity, our life will begin to manifest self-respect because we have nothing to conceal. The way we present ourselves to the outside world matches what we are in our private lives. *Nothing brings about self-respect faster.*

Whenever I meet someone who consistently conveys a respectful attitude toward others, I cannot help but imagine that they are governed by admirable qualities. This is what makes them respectful. On the other hand, when we live with qualities that are less admirable, we will tend to lose self-respect. This is why it becomes difficult to respect others. How can we give what we do not have? In terms of serving others, the qualities that we live by will carry over in how well we take care of our guests.

Building a respectful attitude tip #6...
Learn to be considerate

Be the kind of friend you would want to have.

Being considerate toward others is a genuine sign that a person has an attitude of respect. As guest service representatives, our duty should be to consistently show consideration toward others. This is just common sense. It is difficult to be respectful when we are inconsiderate. Learning to modify this must begin with a change in attitude. *I have found that those who consistently provide outstanding service are well mannered and thoughtful in the way they treat others.* This alone has a major impact in how guests perceive the service. People will always make their first judgment of our Golf Club by how well they have been treated. It can make all the difference in creating guest loyalty.

Building a respectful attitude can happen if we begin to be aware of how we treat others. Do we show kindness and listen to what is being said? Are we patient with a request? We may also want to be aware of our tone of voice when speaking. Do we convey a voice that is obliged to help, or one that expresses a feeling of impatience? These are little indications that will help us to see where improvements may need to take place. The more we examine our behavior toward others, the better off we will be in providing outstanding service.

Building a respectful attitude tip #7...
Learn to become user-friendly

People who honor others with respect also allow themselves to be more approachable. I like to call this being user-friendly. This is an important quality to have if we are to excel in providing excellent service. When our guests sense that we are easily approachable, they will be more likely to rate our service on a higher level. The best way to become user-friendly is to express right from the start a genuine respect for every guest who we will have the pleasure to serve. When guests take note of our pleasant attitude and friendly disposition, they will feel more comfortable to approach us with any additional needs or questions.

Learning to be more approachable to our guests will happen when we honor them by being pleasant and kind. We can show this by expressing a friendly smile and a warm greeting. It is the little gestures that we convey that will give them the green light to approach us. It is our job to make them feel that we are there for them and happy to serve. When guests feel secure enough to approach us and ask for additional assistance, we can be sure that we have created a user-friendly environment for them.

Building a respectful attitude tip #8...
Listening conveys respect

In the last chapter on developing a caring attitude, I went into detail on the importance of listening to others. When we give our full attention, we are expressing a respectful attitude because it conveys that the person we are listening to is important enough to be heard. The power of undivided attention will allow others to express themselves. It also shows that we are considerate. Listening is so much more important than speaking. I frequently say that I never learn anything when I am talking. It is only in listening that true learning can occur. Observe conversations and take note of how much listening actually occurs in the course of a dialogue. It is always astonishing to notice how little is spent on actually listening. From my own observations, I have rarely witnessed one person asking another person a pertinent question during the course of the discussion. *Most of the conversation is focused primarily on statements being thrown back and forth with little inquiry on what had just been stated.*

It is a joy to be in the presence of a person who truly is interested in listening. It is like finding a diamond in the rough. Listeners are a special breed and a pleasure to converse with. They not only make us feel special, but they also allow us to express ourselves in a more meaningful way. *I have observed that it is the listeners of the world who tend to show others the most respect simply because they are not interested in having the spotlight on themselves.* They show respect by allowing the other person to speak. Remember this and others will soon appreciate the respect that you convey to them through your great listening skills!

Attitude #5

The Attitude of Encouraging

Encouragement creates a positive environment for both the guests and the staff.

There is an attitude that can influence and help others to become their best. This attitude has the power to build people up. When we live with this attitude, not only will we make a positive difference in our environment, but we will also assist in bringing out the natural gifts of those around us. The influence that this attitude has on people will give strength and hope to move forward. No other attitude can assist in helping to bring out the best in others quite like this attitude. The attitude I am talking about is encouragement.

How many times have we been in the presence of a person who had a way of bringing out our best? What is it that brought out our finest behavior? More than likely, we were in the presence of a person who had the ability to encourage us either through words or actions. He or she had a way of making us feel better because of their gift of being able to encourage. They were inspirational and looked beyond what we presently were to what we could become. Their genuine care and concern made us realize that their kind words were authentic and without ulterior motives. There were no hidden agendas connected with their encouraging remarks. We knew that this person was honorable and sincere in their words.

When we truly begin to appreciate what encouragement can do for people, we will want to do it more often. *I am convinced that every person needs to be encouraged from time to time.* A positive word can lift people up and assist them to become their best. Using words that build up instead of tear down can make all the difference in a person's life. Words have the power of life and death. The old saying that *"sticks and stones will break my bones but words will never harm me"* has been found to be untrue. Our words can hurt others and tear them down. Every day we have the choice to support others with our choice of words. We can be used as instruments to lift others up or put them down.

When we are serving guests, our words *(along with the tone of our voice)* can make all the difference in how they perceive our service. I have found that the service superstars have a way of communicating in a pleasant tone of voice. Their encouraging attitude and kind words instantly give us the confidence that they are looking out for our best interest. But what about those experiences where the service was marked with a guest service representative who showed no signs of encouragement. I can recall experiences where there would be no friendly greeting or welcoming smile offered. If anything, I felt that I was intruding on their time. There would be no positive sign of encouragement on their part. As a guest I wanted to leave as soon as possible. *Looking back, I can see that these not so pleasant guest service experiences were caused by a lack of encouragement and support.*

> *What men and women need is encouragement.... Instead of always harping on a man's faults, tell him of his qualities. Try to pull him out of his rut of bad habits.*
> --Eleanor H. Porter (Pollyanna)

If encouragement can assist to bring the best out in others, why do we generally have a difficult time doing it? What keeps us from being more encouraging to others? If sincere encouragement is supposed to be proper and helpful, why is it so difficult to show? After much thought, I believe that encouragement is a gift that some are naturally born with; however, those without the gift of encouragement can develop it over time. In the first case scenario, there are some people who have been wonderfully gifted with the attitude of bringing out the best in others. From the start they have had a way of building people up with little or no thought that they are doing it. Encouraging others comes as natural as waking up in the morning. But then there are those who have learned over time the importance of inspiring others and have implemented it into their lives. This should give each of us hope that we can develop a better attitude that brings inspiration to others who may need a helping hand. Before we focus on the traits that will help us to become better encouragers, let's first look at what encouragement can do for others.

The benefits of encouraging

Correction does much, but encouragement will do more.

Over the years I have come to the conclusion that encouragement is the most efficient way to bring the best out in others. I am not talking about empty flattery or saying words that have ulterior motives connected with them. Sincere encouragement has no strings attached. It is important to note that encouraging others can be easily conveyed without a word spoken. It can be a sincere smile or a kind gesture that somehow conveys a feeling that we are on their side. When serving others, it is not so much the words that we use that will express to a person that we are behind them. In many ways it is the way we look at them, or the way we communicate with a friendly gesture that expresses a sense that we are there for them. Something as simple as a pleasant smile will bring encouragement. A friendly hand gesture will also express that we are pleased to see them. Using these small signs will consistently convey to our guests that we care.

Think about the importance of encouraging children during their early formative years. When children have parents or caretakers who understand the importance of encouragement, these children will have a big advantage in their future lives. I have witnessed children who came from homes where words of encouragement were freely given. The parents understood the power of encouragement and it showed in the lives of the children. On the other hand, I have sadly witnessed homes where the normal conversations were embedded with discouraging words and speech that tended to be dispiriting. This of course had an adverse effect in bringing out the best in everyone. In the same manner, if we rarely use words of encouragement, we will have a difficult time bringing out the best in our team members.

One word or a pleasant smile is often enough to lift a person up who simply needed encouragement.

Encouraging words are said to be what sunshine is to flowers. It can be compared to what water is to a man who has just walked twenty miles in a hot desert. To encourage another person is comparable to helping someone who has just fallen to the ground. It shows people that we are there for them and desire that they become their best. Without encouragement, people can slowly wilt like a flower with no water. *When we share a word of affirmation, it is as if we were lending an invisible hand.* With encouragement, there will be times when the results can be instantly seen. It can make a person stand a little taller and walk away with a slight smile on his or her face. A kind word spoken may be all that another person needed at any given moment.

Seven traits commonly found in an attitude of encouragement

We begin to blossom by an encouraging word, but slowly wilt without it.

1. Encouragers support others to be their best

Kind words can be short and easy to speak, but their echoes are truly endless.

The first characteristic found in those who have the gift of encouragement is their ability to bring out the best in others. *This is why encouragers make excellent leaders. They have a way of making others perform at their best.* When we encounter someone who simply loves to encourage, it makes us want to be and do our best. We are attracted to the fact that they believe in us. This one single point becomes a powerful motivator for us to be our absolute best in their presence. It is almost as if we would not want to disappoint them by not trying our best or being on our best behavior. In terms of serving others, *our encouraging attitude will have a positive effect in bringing out their "best guest side" and give them the desire to present their best.* This is because encouragement will always have a way of bringing out the best in everyone, including our guests.

2. Encouragers rarely complain

Those who are lifting the world upward and onward are those who encourage more than criticize.

Think of people who you consider to be great at encouraging others. If you examine their lives more closely, you will notice that they very seldom complain. Encouragers are encouragers because they consistently see the good side of every situation. Instead of seeing the cloudy day, encouragers point to the blue skies behind the clouds. If we are to be better at encouraging others, our first priority is to get rid of all forms of complaining. Not only does grumbling put a monkey wrench in the way we view life, but it also can make us unattractive to be around. How many of us actually enjoy being around those who constantly complain about this and that? Complaining also has a way of making us less encouraging toward others. *The people who encourage can do so because they have learned that whining and faultfinding eventually bring only discontentment into their lives.* If we want to be more encouraging, the first priority is to catch ourselves when we want to grumble and replace it with a heart that is thankful.

3. Encouragers are out to help others

The best help that we can render an afflicted man is not to take away his burden, but to lend him a shoulder, that he may be able to bear the burden.

Of all the positive traits that an encouraging attitude conveys to others, none is more powerful than the impression that we are out to help them. When people sense that we want the best for them, not only will they flourish, but they will also open up and trust us more. In delivering outstanding service to our guests, they will appreciate the feeling that we genuinely want to help them. Guests who sense our sincere desire to give them the best possible service will have all the more confidence in our ability to take care of their needs. They in turn will become loyal and trust our future judgments simply because they know that we care.

A word of encouragement during a failure is worth more than an hour of praise after success.

When we simply want to help others without any ulterior motive, they in turn may eventually become loyal in return. This can be explained by the positive influence of a caring heart. When we care for others, they may automatically begin to care for us. When we want to help others, they in turn want to help us. *In essence, we can sum it up by saying that others will eventually treat us the way that we have treated them.* When we treat our guests with such attributes as kindness, caring, and respect, we will find that they will desire to do the same.

4. Encouragers urge others to better themselves

When we seek to discover the best in others, we somehow bring out the best in ourselves. - William Arthur Ward

Another excellent characteristic that we can find in people who encourage is their ability to persuade others to better themselves. *Encouragers see not what people are but what they can become.* When they converse with another person, they begin to recognize untapped qualities that the person may never have recognized. It is as if these encouragers are gifted with the ability to see the potential in others.

Children learn more from models than from critics.

If we are to improve at encouraging others, we must look beyond what someone is at the present moment and see what he or she can become. By doing this, we will begin to see others in a different light. People will be drawn to us simply because of our accepting attitude. It is as if we are giving them the confidence and conviction that they can change for the better. Where they may have been on the verge of giving up, our encouraging words begin to allow them to have the courage to continue. This is the power of giving encouragement to others.

5. Encouragers are secure in who they are

When we are secure and confident in whom we are, we are much more inclined to encourage others.

The reason for this is that self-assurance allows us the freedom to build others up without wanting the spotlight on ourselves. *Encouragers are confident enough within themselves to pick others up with kind words or a helping hand.* On the other hand are those who try to criticize or put others down in an attempt to feel better about themselves. This self-destructive behavior is an indication that the person is dealing with hidden insecurities. Secure people have no need to judge or speak poorly of others in order to lift themselves up. On the contrary, people who enjoy lifting others up exhibit a self-confidence that allows this to occur. In reality, it is the encouragers of the world who are most secure in whom they are. That is why they have no need to criticize others. This will play a positive role in our relationship with others. *Remember, the more secure a person is, the more likely he or she will be able to freely encourage others.*

6. Encouragers never stop growing

*Those who bring sunshine into the lives of others
cannot keep it from themselves.*

Another trait that we will find in people who encourage is their desire to continue to learn. Because of their desire to see others reach their full potential in life, they carry this conviction into their own personal lives. This desire to see others grow is a benefit that will motivate an encourager to become his or her best. This aspiration to learn is a characteristic that identifies those who enjoy building others up. *Without realizing it, they have developed a healthy inner drive to better themselves simply because their outward attitude of encouraging others has positively affected them!* When we truly see the potential in others, we cannot help but want to use our gifts and talents to the best of our ability. This is the reason that people with an attitude of encouragement continue to grow. Their desire to help others has motivated their own lives.

7. Encouragers are excited when others achieve

We need to applaud the accomplishments of others, recognize their successes, and encourage them in their pursuits. By helping others, everybody wins.

Those who have a genuine attitude of encouragement express joy when others achieve a certain goal or accomplishment. Because of their good nature, encouragers carry no jealousy or insecurities. *They are happy when people succeed and are not threatened by the triumphs and successes of others.* When our attitude is one where we can rejoice in the victories of others, we can be confident that we are self-secure within ourselves. Because of the self-confidence that goes along with an encouraging attitude, these people are secure enough to not have to compare themselves with others. Being secured with who they are, they do not feel better about themselves when others fail or fall short of a goal. *On the contrary, they enjoy seeing others succeed. This is the true sign of someone who genuinely has the gift of encouragement.* Another benefit is that it makes people want the encourager to succeed as well. Because encouragers never show jealousy or animosity, others cannot help but want the best for them.

The secret of creating a great guest service team

By now I hope that we can understand the positive influences that encouragement has on other people. If we are to build a great guest service team, it is paramount that we create an environment where each member of the team is encouraged to do their best. *The best managers understand that positive reinforcement will always outperform negative words of discouragement.* When a leader leads with the best interest of others, he or she will continually offer words of encouragement. Instead of looking for little faults or minor mistakes, the best leaders have a way of communicating that consistently brings out the best in others. These managers have a way of relating to their team that both inspires and motivates each person to do his or her best. They use their words carefully and never come across in a rude or impolite manner. When managers consistently work toward bringing out the best in their team, the team will show their appreciation by doing their best on the job.

I am always baffled when hearing accounts where the leadership consistently uses dispiriting words in an effort to motivate those under them. In reality, this approach will only backfire for those who communicate in ill-mannered ways. *This is because people will never want to do their best when they have been disrespected. They may do what needs to be done to get the job finished, but their hearts will never be in it.*

On the other hand, when management genuinely cares about the welfare of those who work for them, the attitude of the environment will change for the better. When people are encouraged and treated in a manner that is both respectful and honoring, the responsibilities of the job will take on new meaning. This is the beauty of encouraging. *It gives employees the desire to want to do their best simply because they have been treated with dignity.* This also creates a work environment where everyone begins to build each other up. This positive atmosphere becomes a chain reaction that eventually will have an effect on the way our guests are treated. *Exceptional guest service then becomes a by-product and reflection of the way management has treated their employees.* This is the secret of creating a great guest service team.

Attitude #6
The Attitude of Thankfulness
Guests who feel appreciated will rate our service higher.

One of the secrets for living a more fulfilling life is being able to consistently live with a heart of gratitude. There is something that changes our whole outlook on life when we capture the ability to appreciate the simple gift called life. No other attitude has a way of filling us with delight as does capturing the attitude of being thankful. Not only will it affect every area of our life, but it will also make us more attractive to be around. Being in the presence of those who are thankful can be comparable to a peaceful sunset across a calm lake. We watch as the sun slowly fades away and in complete silence we sense the beauty of it. In the same manner, when we are in the presence of someone who radiates appreciation for simply being alive, we silently sense the beauty that it portrays.

Thankfulness is never anything that we can buy or barter for. Just look into the lives of thousands of affluent people throughout the pages of history and we will discover that wealth has never brought lasting happiness. The reason for this is because contentment and gratitude grows within the quietness of our hearts. No amount of material gain will purchase it for us. Temporary treasures eventually fade and we begin to search again. I like to compare it to a man who is dying of thirst and begins to drink salt water from the sea. Before long he becomes thirsty again, but this time his thirst has increased all the more. In the same way, trying to capture a thankful heart by collecting material objects will eventually leave us wanting more.

So what does this have to do with guest services and being able to deliver outstanding service to our guests? How exactly does having a heart of appreciation connect with serving others? I believe it is one of the best attitudes that we can have for becoming guest service superstars. *When we truly live a life of appreciation, it will carry over in the way that we treat others, especially those we serve.* This is the advantage of living with a thankful heart. When we start to live with an attitude of gratitude, we will begin to improve in every other area of our lives, including our service to others. But before moving on, it's important that we understand the guest's perspective when he or she is shown appreciation.

Why appreciation appeals to our guests

"Gratitude is not only the greatest of virtues, but the parent of all others." -- Marcus Cicero

I remember coming across a story about a young man who had been fired from an ice cream parlor. One of his duties was to say thank you whenever he handed an ice cream cone to a guest. The owner of the parlor understood the power of appreciation and made it a part of the job description for each employee who served the ice cream. The owner finally had to let the young man go because of his forgetfulness to say thank you.

I relate this story because I am convinced that guests will always rate our service higher if we show them our appreciation in having done business with us. I am also convinced that the Golf Club that consistently shows appreciation will have an advantage. Other clubs may be able to match in regard to the facility amenities, but what will always separate and make a club stand out will be the appreciation that is consistently conveyed to each guest.

Let's look at an example from the restaurant business. Let's say that I was to open a family restaurant, and the area already had eight similar restaurants. I am pretty sure that the food in each restaurant would all taste similar and the prices would all be competitive. *What I would focus on the most would be to hire people who had hospitable personalities. They would have to be welcoming and excited to be working at the restaurant. I would also look for the six attitudes described in this book. I would want them to be friendly, enthused, caring, respectful, encouraging, and thankful.*

If I could find people who had all of these qualities there would be no question that this new restaurant would be an instant hit. *Guests would want to come back simply because of the way that we made them feel.* More importantly, we would make it a habit to show each guest our sincere appreciation for visiting our restaurant. Before leaving, I would want to make sure every guest knew that we were thankful that they chose us over the other restaurants.

The power of appreciation can never be underestimated. Think of the times that we may have done something nice for someone and soon forgot about it. A few days later we receive a card in the mail with a note of appreciation for what we did. Taken by surprise, we feel overwhelmed that someone would take the time to actually send us a card. How did it make us feel? More than likely it felt good to have been appreciated. This gesture of appreciation also gave us an inner desire to want to help this person in the future. *In the same manner, when we show appreciation to our guests, they in turn want to support us.* We need to understand that everyone enjoys being appreciated. This is why having an attitude of thankfulness is so beneficial if we want to become guest service superstars.

A few years ago my wife and I surprised our three children at Christmas with a little puppy. He was a cute little fellow with fluffy white curls, and we named him Cuddles. It didn't take long for us to fall in love with Cuddles because of his loving ways. Anyone who has ever had a dog can relate to what I am saying. As I reflect on Cuddles, I have come to realize that one of his most likable traits is how he can display his appreciation toward us. When we take off to run errands, guess who is always waiting by the front window for our return? His excitement and appreciation in seeing us return can sometimes be overwhelming. With Cuddles jumping and wagging his tail at us, we cannot help but feel loved. It is this "secret weapon" of being thankful that has won our utmost loyalty to our little dog.

Like Cuddles, we too can win the hearts of our guests when we show them how much we appreciate their support. Unlike Cuddles, we do not have to jump up and down when we welcome our guests, *but how about giving a friendly and hospitable greeting to convey how much we appreciate their support?* This small gesture of showing our guests appreciation is without question one of the best gifts we can offer them. But remember that expressing thankfulness must be sincere and from the heart. I am sure that you can recall moments as a guest when you were given a somewhat expressionless thank-you that did not seem real. *More than likely it was spoken out of duty rather than from the heart.*

The worst poverty is produced by a life empty of gratitude.

The two types of thank-you

I have found that the expression of a thank you given after being served by a guest service representative falls under two basic categories. The first category is when service representatives express a thank you simply because it falls under their job description. *This type of thank you is usually forgotten before the guest reaches the exit door.* As guests, we can easily spot this thank you because of the way it was expressed and the lack of genuineness conveyed. It would be similar to the tone of voice received if we were to ask where the restrooms were located.

The second category of receiving a thank you is much more attractive because of its sincerity. *We as guests can sense through the pleasant tone of voice and appreciative smile that this expression was sincere.* When this occurs, we walk away feeling appreciated. The power conveying a sincere thank you toward others not only attracts, but it also makes guests want to continue to support us. Once we truly understand this, we will see more guests wanting to play our facility.

Staying away from complaining

"What if you gave someone a gift, and they neglected to thank you for it — would you be likely to give them another? Life is the same way. In order to attract more of the blessings that life has to offer, you must truly appreciate what you already have."
-- Ralph Marston - Writer

One of the best benefits we will receive by having an *attitude of gratitude* is that it not only gives others a good feeling inside, but it also makes us healthier. Thankfulness has a way of keeping us overflowing with inner contentment. I have found that those who are most content in life are people who consistently show appreciation. On the other side are those who give the impression of never being content. Their most prevalent attitude tends to be one of complaining. Not only are they rarely satisfied about most things, but they also show little appreciation toward others. I believe that the main reason that it is difficult for these complainers to show thankfulness is because of the constant grumbling that has eroded any signs of joy. *When we begin to moan and complain, we will soon find that it becomes more difficult to appreciate life. Grumbling has a way of whittling away a thankful heart.* Complaining has to be the number one roadblock for obtaining an attitude of appreciation. No other attitude can destroy us like complaining.

The best antidote for staying away from a complaining attitude is to simply avoid it altogether. I realize this suggestion sounds too straightforward, but the only thing that will continue to feed this destructive attitude is to continue to do it. Complaining may start small and innocently, but over time it can affect every other attitude. I believe it needs to be avoided like the plague. Nothing good will ever come when we live a life of constant complaining.

Chapter 3
Understanding Great Service
What It Takes to Produce Five-Star Service...

Five-star guest service is meeting and then exceeding the guest's expectations.

Every person in the world will play the role of a guest throughout his or her life. From early on each of us becomes acquainted with being the guest and having others wait on us. No matter where we go, we are always prepared to take on the role of the guest and be served by another person. Look at a typical week and we discover just how much time is spent on being a guest. We go to the grocery store and we automatically become the guest. We go to the dentist and again become the guest. Head to the bank and what do you know, we are given the role of being the guest again. No matter where we go, we are always bestowed with the title of the guest. For those who love to go to the marketplace on a regular basis, they will live most of their waking days playing the role of a guest. Their lives will be lived as guests waiting to be served.

When we look at the hundreds of experiences that we have had as a guest, we have also discovered that some people are better at serving than others. Every once in a while we come across a service representative who had served us in an outstanding manner. We walk away feeling that this person went beyond the call of duty and gave us exceptional service. We may also remember a few times where someone was serving us who did not seem to enjoy what he or she was doing. We felt uncomfortable and left feeling that the service was poor. But for the most part, our daily experiences of being served fall in the average category. We walk away soon forgetting the experience. The effort that the service representative gave appeared to be more like a job description that was being followed. The smile (if there was one) and the thank you (if there was one) tended to be without much expression. It might as well have been a robot that was helping us.

More often than not, we find that service in America is typically average. As mentioned, we will have memorable moments when we will be served by a guest service superstar. But on average, being served by others usually gives us the impression that the service representative is simply following protocol. I have also found that average service has no boundaries. It can appear at a place where we would expect excellent service. We have all had moments of looking forward to great service only to be greeted with average or below average service. On the other hand, I have been pleasantly surprised to be given five-star service when all I really expected was average or below average service.

In all of these cases, I have discovered that receiving exceptional service cannot be measured from outside appearances. This is because five-star service can only come as a result of a person genuinely caring about the guest. If a service representative is not serving from a sincere and caring heart, more than likely the service will be perceived as average. Remember this important statement:

"Five-star service can only occur when we care about meeting our guest's immediate needs. Without a caring heart, guest service simply becomes following a job description."

When we try to make the experience for the guest as pleasant as possible, he or she will perceive the service provided as first-rate. It does not matter if the service revolves around selling a product or providing a service. When we serve with the best intentions for the guest, he or she will view our service as excellent. There are no restrictions in what we may be providing for the guest. It could be anything from trying to make a multi-million dollar sale to serving someone in a restaurant. In both cases, guests will perceive our service as being excellent when they feel that we had their best interest in mind.

Guests will perceive our service as being excellent when they feel that we had their best interest in mind.

If I had to summarize five-star service, I would state that it is caring more about the guest than simply making a sale or following a job description. When we begin to serve from the heart, they cannot help but notice that we are on their side. They will also sense that we are thinking about their needs. This is serving with the right intentions. Let's now look at six thoughts that will assist in offering excellent Golf Club service for your guests.

1. Five-star service is being courteous

Being courteous to our guests should be a given for every person on your staff. It would seem only logical that anyone who is working out in front with guests would be hospitable. But is this always the case? How many experiences have each of us had where we felt that the person serving us was unfriendly or inconsiderate? I am sure that we can all recall moments as a guest where we felt the person serving us was unwelcoming. If providing five-star service is ever going to take place in a Golf Club, the first step is to have employees who are courteous to every guest. This is a necessity, and without it a Golf Club will soon become extinct.

I am always surprised when someone is placed out in front who also tends to show an unfriendly attitude. The first thought that crosses my mind is why the Golf Club would put someone with an unwelcoming attitude out in front with guests. If guests are the people who will eventually determine the fate of the club, it would seem only logical to place the friendliest people out in front with guests. This is why fitting staff members in the correct job position can make all the difference in how guests will perceive your Golf Club. The reputation of a club can be stained because of discourteous people working with the public. It only takes one team member to make your operation look bad if he or she is consistently being inconsiderate to guests.

It only takes one team member to make your operation look bad if he or she is consistently being inconsiderate to guests.

Allow me to relate a story regarding service at a dentist office. For two years the business was slowly losing guests. The two owners were both excellent dentists and had fine reputations. The location and marketing were also on track. Being unable to find the problem, the owners decided to hire a consultant to come in and figure out why they were losing guests. After a few days of investigation, the consultant had found the source of their troubles. After observing the day-to-day operation in the dentist office, the consultant discovered that the reason guests were not coming back was due to the unfriendly personality of the front desk manager. Guests did not want to come back simply because they did not feel comfortable around her. It was her way of treating them disrespectfully that made them look for another dentist. Eventually the problem was resolved when the owners finally replaced her with a friendlier manager. In a short time the business started to pick up and grow.

In my own experiences I have watched how guests have been treated by people who were supposed to be there to serve them. Many times I have walked away wondering if the Golf Club realized the potential damage that an unfriendly team member may be causing by his or her unwelcoming attitude. I refer to this as having a hole in the ship. On a large ship everyone has a job to do. Some are in charge of mopping the deck while others are in charge of handling the large sails. There are those on the ship who are in charge of keeping the ship going in the right direction. Each person has a specific task in making the ship perform at its best. But let's imagine that one person had the responsibility of keeping water out of the bottom of the ship. One day the ship begins to tilt to the left. After investigating, the crew discovers that the person who was in charge of keeping water out of the bottom of the ship is sleeping with the large bucket in his hand. Water has seeped in and is almost up to everyone's knees. Waking the sleeping man, they inform him that the ship is tilting because he is not doing his job. A few days later this happens again and the crew again discovers that the man is sleeping. They again have to awaken him and inform him that the ship will sink if he does not perform his duty of keeping the water out.

In the same way, it can take only one person to sink a Golf Club if he or she is not being considerate to guests. This is what had happened at the dentist office. A club can eventually weaken when there are people out in front who are in the habit of repelling guests. Being courteous to others must happen continually if we are ever to perform five-star service.

2. Five-star service is being urgent

I like to think of providing excellent service as a mission that demands urgency. By this I mean that we look at serving others as something that is important to them and must be treated as such. We see our contact with guests as a significant and pressing matter that needs to be resolved in a timely and professional manner. *Those who are the superstars of guest service serve in such a way that gives the impression that the guest's request is the most important concern in the world.* By listening intently and expressing that we will take care of the issue as soon as possible automatically gives the impression that this guest is a VIP and will be treated as such.

On the other hand, I have witnessed where the service representative had given the impression to the guest that his or her request was an interruption. This *"you are bothering me"* mentality will ward off guests in no time. Our job is to treat every request as if it were the most important request in the world.

Our job is to treat every request as if it were the most important request in the world.

79

Our guests will quickly take note of this and appreciate how willing we were in taking care of their immediate need. If we are to consistently provide excellent service, *it is vital that we give the impression that the guest's request is urgent and in need of immediate attention.* Once we have done this, it is now our turn to follow up and take care of the issue.

3. Five-star service is a team effort

The sky truly is the limit when a Golf Club has a team that is passionate about creating great service. This is because each team member plays a key role in how well the service will be perceived. It is important to understand that every staff member is a reflection of not only the Golf Club, but also of each other. When we have a team that is committed to providing outstanding service, we then will begin to build each other up through our mutual goals. But what happens if we are surrounded with people that do not have the same passion and fervor that we may have for giving our guests exceptional service? What would occur if we worked at a Golf Club that simply did not make guest service a high priority? *More than likely we would have little support and encouragement in our desire to create exceptional service.* This is why it is important to hire the right people who enjoy serving people. When this occurs, we will then find ourselves surrounded with a supporting cast who will not only provide brilliant service, but also encourage us as well. In order to provide five-star service, we must first start by creating a team that is excited to serve.

4. Five-star service is about training

The best service Golf Clubs who consistently produce five-star service make training a top priority. Along with hiring the right people who enjoy serving others, these Golf Clubs realize the importance and benefits of education. For the most part, the majority of guest service training in America is taught in a one-shot deal. It may occur during the hiring process or during the first few days on the job. But if we are serious about producing outstanding service, consistent training must become a part of the Golf Club. It is up to us to decide how much time should be devoted to this instruction. This will not only improve the service to the guest, but it will also reinforce our belief that five-service is a top priority.

5. Five-star service is in our tone of voice

Guests will read our willingness to serve them by the tone of voice that we use. Our tone is much more important than the words that we say. This is especially true when we are talking on the telephone. If we are to offer five-star service, our words must be spoken in a pleasant tone of voice. How many times can we recall contacting a Golf Club over the telephone and hanging up sensing that service was not a high priority on their list? How is it that we came to this conclusion? More than likely is was the tone of voice that was used by the person who had represented the Golf Club. What is startling is that we can have a negative opinion of a Golf Club simply because of one team member who had an impolite tone of voice.

We can have a negative opinion of a Golf Club simply because of one team member who had an impolite tone of voice.

Whether we are on the telephone or in person, our tone of voice is really what is being heard the most. If we want to give our guests outstanding service, it is important to be aware of how we articulate and convey our words.

6. Five-star service is really about enjoying it

In order to give great service we need to enjoy serving others. By enjoying the process of helping others, we will be better at producing five-star service. I believe that one of the best qualities found in guest service superstars is that they thoroughly enjoy serving people.

*One of the best qualities found in guest service superstars is that they
thoroughly enjoy serving people.*

This alone makes it all the more effortless in delivering exceptional
service. When we truly enjoy serving others, our occupation becomes
less of a job and more of a profession.

What Makes a Super Team?

*A super guest service team has certain qualities that make them
consistently produce five-star service.*

Why is it that some Golf Clubs can flourish while others tend to never
take off? What is the difference in why some clubs have a way to
consistently produce outstanding service while others simply get by?
Is there a secret that these successful Golf Clubs have that allows them
to perform at their best time and again? Looking more closely, we will
find that there is one single factor that allows some clubs to succeed.
This feature that separates these Golf Clubs from the rest of the pack is
the people. It is what I have termed *a super team* who understands
what five-star service is all about. These Golf Clubs have a strong
belief that business is first and foremost about serving others.

*These Golf Clubs have a strong belief that business is first and
foremost about serving others.*

For them, it does not matter what product or service is being provided
for the guest. What does matter is that the guest feels valued and
appreciated. These super teams have the mindset that the product or
service being provided is secondary to the real goal of being able to
connect and build trust with each guest. Their ultimate goal is to focus
on making guests walk away *with the desire to want to return.* Great
service can only occur if we serve from the platform of genuinely
caring about the needs of our guests.

Great service can only occur if we serve from the platform of genuinely caring about the needs of our guests.

The super teams of guest service look at every business transaction as an opportunity to win guests by the service being provided. Super teams understand that anyone can basically match the product and price that they are presenting to the guest. But what sets them apart is their strong belief that no one will match their service. This is what makes them stand out above the rest. These experts in guest service focus primarily on making guests want to return.

These experts in guest service focus primarily on making guests want to return.

They will do whatever it takes to give the perception that their service will not be matched. This alone is what makes these Golf Clubs stay ahead of the game. When we take a closer look and analyze these successful Golf Clubs, we will find certain qualities that set them apart and help them in maintaining a supportive team. On the outside they may look similar to other Golf Clubs, but under a microscope we will find something quite different. Looking closer we will find a strong team that not only can deliver excellent service, but also build each other up to become the best that they can be on the job. Let's now turn our attention and discover six qualities that make a super guest service team.

1. A super team first serves each other

The first noticeable difference in great service teams is their willingness to serve each other. How well they serve guests is a reflection of how well they serve each other. The team is strong because they understand that everyone working together will produce better results.

The team is strong because they understand that everyone working together will produce better results.

There are no individuals in super guest service teams. Each person is there to serve. It does not matter if the service is for a guest or a fellow staff member. The mentality is that the job is simply about serving. Everyone has the same goal. Titles and positions take a backseat when it comes to serving others. When everyone on the team serves each other, they only reinforce the mission of delivering great service to the guest. This serving each other also makes the team forget about competing against each other. They view everyone as working together with the ultimate goal of delivering great service to the guest.

2. A super team enjoys their profession

Have you ever known someone who truly enjoyed his or her job? More than likely it was due to the environment in which they worked. I have found that most people who enjoy going to work do so because of the people that they work with. Everyone tends to work toward a common cause and the feeling of harmony permeates throughout the entire operation. In these positive environments what we will discover are a group of people who truly enjoy what they do. They enjoy the challenge as well as the camaraderie that has developed among the team. Most people who enjoy their occupation do so because of the supportive atmosphere that is felt.

Most people who enjoy their occupation do so because of the supportive atmosphere that is felt.

On the other hand, Golf Clubs that lack five-star service have less harmony among its team members. This not only affects the service offered, but also makes team members less satisfied with their occupation.

3. A super team believes in continual learning

Super guest service teams have another quality that sets them apart from others. This is their continual desire to learn. These teams are motivated to educate themselves through various avenues. This is one of the reasons that they are continually motivated and fresh with new ideals. When we are consistently learning, we will avoid being stagnant on the job. This is one of the many benefits of providing training programs within the Golf Club. It allows team members to grow and expand their knowledge. On the other hand, a lack of motivation and decrease in providing outstanding service can be a reflection of being inactive in the desire to learn. By systematically getting involved in training programs that can assist in motivating the staff, we will soon find the service improving.

4. A super team is experts in their field

Super guest service teams have a high degree of expertise in their particular field. They understand what their position calls for and have become true professionals on the job. Guests who are served by them quickly recognize that these people are specialist in their profession. This is one telling trait found in super teams. They are true experts, and this alone will project to the guest inner confidence that the service being received will be outstanding. When guests sense that a dedicated expert is serving them, they walk away feeling that the service was wonderful.

5. A super team allows for mistakes

Another quality found in super teams is their ability to show grace when mistakes are made. By allowing room for human errors that will occur from time to time, it gives everyone on the team the freedom from always feeling under pressure. When an attitude of grace permeates within the team, it makes everyone less judgmental when a mistake has happened.

When an attitude of grace permeates within the team, it makes everyone less judgmental when a mistake has happened.

85

What these super guest service teams recognize is that everyone is bound to make a blunder from time to time. Having this acceptance makes everyone feel less pressure, and also gives team members the assurance that others will not jump at the opportunity to criticize them when a human slip-up has occurred. Because of this grace-filled environment, the team has learned to build each other up and be less critical when mistakes are made. We will always build a better service team by conveying a sense of grace when correcting a mistake.

6. A super team never forgets its mission

The final quality found in teams that consistently produce outstanding service is the firm belief in their ultimate mission. They never forget that serving others is why they exist. With this type of mentality, it is no wonder that these Golf Clubs consistently produce five-star service. Unlike many Golf Clubs that have no focused mission, these successful Golf Clubs continually remind their team that the guest's satisfaction is the basis for their continuation. They never stop focusing on the fact that guests are the reason for their existence. Because of this strong commitment to guest service, the super teams are consistently reminded to first and foremost take care of the guest. This alone makes all the difference in why these Golf Clubs deliver five-star service time and again.

What Attracts Guests?

The end result of providing outstanding service is gaining guests who will want to return and tell their friends about their outstanding experience.

If I were to pinpoint the goal of every service campaign, it is simply to give our guests the best of what we have to offer. It would be going all out in making their experience as pleasant as possible. The result would be creating guest loyalty and having them tell others about our great service. I have come to the conclusion that every Golf Club in the world is either attracting guests or repelling guests. It eventually becomes one or the other. Our guests will be able to sense right away if we are giving them excellent service or if we are just going through the motions simply for a paycheck. If we are to be successful in our profession, it is imperative that we understand that certain behaviors can be a magnet in drawing guests back. On the other hand, there are certain actions that are detrimental in winning guest loyalty. In order to provide five-star service, we must distinguish between the two. I am convinced that great service is a result of having the right people who understand how guests think and feel.

Great service is a result of hiring the right people who understand how guests think and feel.

If we are to have an advantage, it is important to place people in the right position that will be able to utilize their gifts. Some Golf Clubs have been fortunate in hiring service superstars who work out in front with guests. These superstars understand people and are aware of what attracts guests. Not only do they create a friendly and welcoming atmosphere, but also become like magnets that continually draw people back again and again.

So what does it take to attract guests and make them want to tell others about our superb service? What do the superstars do that separates them from the rest? My goal throughout this book is to give each reader an overall picture of what delivers five-star service time and again. But in order to do this we must understand some basic premises that will help us attract more guests. Following are six tips that win every time.

1. Attentiveness attracts guests

The first basic lesson in guest service 101 is to simply pay attention to our guests. Giving them our full attention is absolutely critical if we are to deliver five-star service. Without proper attention, our guests will perceive us as unprofessional. They will look at our service as average to below average. It is vital that we understand that guests expect to be noticed when making contact with us.

It is vital that we understand that guests expect to be noticed when making contact with us.

This is one of the allurements in playing the role of a guest. Our role as service representatives is to acknowledge their presence and then be available for them. In far too many cases, guests are ignored and not given the proper greeting that should go along with excellent service.

The best way to welcome a guest is to acknowledge them through a smile or a simple greeting.

The best way to welcome a guest is to acknowledge them through a smile or a simple greeting.

Maybe we could ask them if they need any assistance or to let them know that we are available if they have any additional questions. *The important point to understand is that being attentive will convey that we are ready and willing to serve them.* Remember to also be considerate when greeting a guest. Avoid being overbearing. No one appreciates an aggressive approach. If we are to draw our guests back, we must consistently use discretion and respect their privacy.

2. Trust attracts guests

What is the number one quality that a Golf Club must have in order to create guest loyalty? What one trait will automatically make our guests tell others about their experience at our club? The answer is trust. It is only when guests trust us that will allow them to spread the word about our excellent service.

It is only when guests trust us that will allow them to spread the word about our excellent service.

Without this trust, our guests will find another club to patronize. Trust comes as a result of showing others that we care more about them than simply making a sale. Caring about our guests will give them a reason to put their trust in us. Without caring, trust will never occur.

Without caring, trust will never occur.

In the same manner, loyalty occurs when guests have the confidence that we will give them the best service possible. They trust that we will be honest and deliver great service time and again. This also will give them a reason to tell others about our service. It is important to understand that guests will never tell others about our Golf Club if they do not trust us. This is because the guest is in essence putting his or her reputation on the line when recommending us to others. In order to do this they must have the confidence that we will give excellent service to those they recommend. Without this belief, our guests will more than likely not recommend us.

I had an unpleasant experience a few years ago with a certain business that I had highly recommended to friends. I received a product at a fair price and suggested this business. To make a long story short, my friends went to this place and had poor service and an overall bad experience. When they told me about this, I personally felt embarrassed that I had recommended this place to my friends. I had put my reputation on the line in recommending this business. It was an awkward experience but taught me the importance of being more cautious in who I would recommend in the future.

3. Being knowledgeable attracts guests

How many times have you entered a business only to be served by a person who did not have the answers to your questions? This happens all of the time. We seek information either in person or over the telephone and are put on hold or told to come back for the answer. In order to produce five-star service, it is paramount that we are knowledgeable about the product or service being provided. Guests will always rate our service lower when we are not knowledgeable about the product or service being provided.

Guests will always rate our service lower when we are not knowledgeable about the product or service being provided.

There will be moments when we will be stumped on a question, but overall our knowledge must be strong if we are to give a favorable impression to our guests. They expect us to be experts in our field. When they perceive that we are educated and well informed, they will feel secure enough to trust us and continue to either do business in the future or tell others about our outstanding service.

4. Patience attracts guests

Have you ever been in the role as a guest and were being served by someone who displayed amazing patience with you? Not only did they go the extra mile, but they also went far beyond what was expected. Patient and serene people have a way of drawing us in because of their calm and relaxed approach to life. When a service representative who displays a calm disposition serves us, it gives a sense of confidence that we are in good hands. On the other hand, when we sense that the service representative is frazzled or exhausted, this somehow makes us less confident that we are receiving great service.

Being patient attracts guests simply because it conveys that we are there to serve them. When we are patient with others, it expresses that we are not trying to rush them. This is important because guests never want to feel like a number.

Guests never want to feel like a number.

Of course this is not to say that we are to be slow in serving them. On the contrary, we want to offer them the best and most efficient service without giving them the impression that we are impatient. In the end, we will discover that showing our guests a patient and calm disposition will make them want to tell others about the professional courtesy that was shown to them.

5. *"We are there for you"* attracts guests

The superstars in guest service recognize the importance of making their guests feel important. This is because every guest is important. If we are to have our guests return, it is essential that we make them feel significant. We must express that we are there for them. As mentioned earlier in this chapter, when we show our guests attentiveness, they in turn will want to return. In the same way, we must convey to our guests that our goal is to meet their immediate needs in the best possible manner. By giving our undivided attention and making every guest feel important, we will not only attract them by our service, but also give them a legitimate reason to tell others about our excellent service. Remember that guests are important because they will eventually determine our success or failure. Without guests, our Golf Club would slowly sink.

There is a second and more significant reason that we should regard our guests as important. More significantly, we must remember that each guest that we have the honor to serve is a fellow human being just like us. This alone should be reason enough to view each person as important. When we capture this principle, our service and relationships will instantly improve for the better.

6. A smile attracts guests

Guests first and foremost will sense how well we serve by our greeting to them. If we are to give a great first impression, it is essential that we express a friendly smile from the start. Smiling is one of the best ways to attract others, yet it is often overlooked. If we were to reflect back on this past week as a guest, how many times did others start out with a smile? More than likely it happened infrequently. But if we are to attract guests, it is vital that we begin with a friendly greeting. This is a great icebreaker and will express to our guests that we are willing to serve them with enjoyment

In my first book on guest service, I spoke about the positive influence that a smile can have on others. I became so convinced of this that I entitled the book *Service Starts With a Smile.* When all is said and done, our guests will first and foremost remember how friendly and welcoming we were toward them. They will be attracted to us because of the respect and friendliness that we have shown them. We must remember that our guests are first judging us on the basis of how friendly we were toward them.

Remember that our guests are first judging us on the basis of how friendly we were toward them.

Start off with a friendly smile and you will begin in the right direction in producing five-star service.

What Keeps Guests Away?

If we are to attract guests, there are certain behaviors that we must avoid at all costs.

If we were to really think about it, every Golf Club basically has *one shot* at winning a guest. This "moment of truth" happens when a new guest makes contact with our Golf Club. This contact can occur either in person or over the telephone. How they perceive our service in the first few minutes is likely to stay with them for a long time. In far too many cases, guests never return because of a bad experience during the first initial contact. This of course can be unfair and unreasonable from a logical standpoint. To make a judgment based on one experience does not seem fair.

To make a judgment based on one experience does not seem fair.

But sad to say, this occurs more often than we would like it to happen. And what is worse is that the unsatisfied guest will usually tell others about the poor experience which came from one bad incident. Maybe one of the reasons for this unfair judgment is that we are given so many available options to choose from. If a guest is not satisfied with the service, there are nine other Golf Clubs to choose from. This can be good or this can be bad. It all depends on whether or not we would like more guests. But if we want to excel and make an impact at our Golf Club, we need to view the competition as a motivator for improving our overall service.

Instead of looking at the competition as a roadblock, we should see it as an opportunity to improve on our services. This is because offering the best service will always win out in the end. There will always be those who are price conscious or stay with one Golf Club for a number of reasons, but that should not stop us in wanting to give our guests the absolute finest service that we can offer. If we are to provide outstanding service in the midst of other Golf Clubs competing for the same guest loyalty, it is vital that we avoid a few minor mistakes that keep clubs from reaching their potential. I am convinced through many years of playing the role of a guest that many Golf Clubs have never reached their potential simply because they continue to make the same mistakes year after year.

Many Golf Clubs have never reached their potential simply because they continue to make the same mistakes year after year.

For some unexplainable reason, these underachieved Golf Clubs fall into the same habits that keeps guests at bay. It is as if they exist for the sole purpose of fending off guests. But it does not have to stay this way. If these clubs would simply change a few harmful habits that scare guests off, they could begin to make some positive strides toward better service. Let's look at four detrimental behaviors that need to be avoided at all costs.

1. Guests won't come back because of apathy

The number one disease that can destroy any Golf Club is when apathy takes root. This can be recognized as boredom and a lack of concern for the guest. As guests, we can sense the disease of apathy as soon as we make contact with a Golf Club that has become unconcerned.

As guests, we can sense the disease of apathy as soon as we make contact with a Golf Club that has become unconcerned.

We get the feeling that nobody really cares. As guests, we sense a lack of motivation and feel more like an interruption when we enter the door. This apathetic attitude is comparable to a ship ready to sink. If we are going to stay afloat, it is imperative that we never fall into the trap of indifference to the guest. We must guard our belief that the guest is the most important person on our premise.

The guest is the most important person on our premise.

The moment that we lose this belief becomes the moment that we begin to allow a root of indifference to settle in. Many Golf Clubs either have lost the vision of the importance of the guest or frankly have never captured it. What eventually occurs in these visionless clubs is that they eventually surround themselves with likeminded people who maintain the status quo. In many regards, we will find that apathy eventually attracts apathy.

Apathy eventually attracts apathy.

If we are to be at our best in attracting guests, it is important to maintain the belief that serving others must be at the forefront.

2. Guests won't come back because of poor listening

Poor service involves so much more than simply forgetting to smile or becoming apathetic. When we talk about poor service, we are referring to the overall experience that we have created for the guest. In order to perform five-star service, we must think of serving as a full-time opportunity to give our best to others. When our guests recognize that we have given them our best, they will want to return. But when they sense that we are just attempting to get by, they will eventually find a new Golf Club to patronize. For the most part, Golf Clubs that perform poor service never recognize it.

For the most part, Golf Clubs that perform poor service never recognize it.

In their mind's eye they consider their service to be above average. What occurs is that these poor service clubs never really listen to the guest. Because they do not seek out the opinion of the guest, they continue to give poor service. This problem occurs as a result of not listening. The Golf Clubs who make the most mistakes do so because they refuse to listen to their guests

The Golf Clubs who make the most mistakes do so because they refuse to listen to their guests.

On the other hand, the intelligent Golf Clubs understand that their greatest resource is the input given by their guests. This is the key to their success. If we are to keep our guests, it is vital that we keep our ears open and listen more closely.

3. Guests won't come back because of inattentiveness

One of the main attractions of being a guest is the attention that is given. For the most part, guests expect to be noticed and given the proper consideration that great five-star service always provides. I am always amazed when playing the role of a guest and experiencing how frequently inattentiveness occurs. If service representatives only understood how little it takes to show a guest proper acknowledgement, I am sure that it would happen more often. A kind smile or a friendly gesture would satisfy the majority of guests. Every once in a while I come across someone who understands the power of attentiveness. He or she will offer a warm greeting and within seconds make me feel welcomed. This little gesture is a key to consistently provide five-star service.

If we are to create an atmosphere that projects great service to our guests, it is paramount that we make them feel welcomed. Within each of us is a desire to feel accepted and received by others. When we offer a friendly greeting, we are in essence giving our guests a feeling of belonging.

When we offer a friendly greeting, we are in essence giving our guests a feeling of belonging.

This alone can have a profound effect on how they will perceive our service. In order to do this, we must be attentive and available when needed. On the other hand, when we show ourselves to be withdrawn and reserved, our guests will not feel as welcomed and accepted. By offering a warm greeting, we will do wonders in not only drawing our guests in, but also give them a sense that we sincerely care.

4. Guests won't come back because of a lack of trust

When speaking to others I like to ask what is the number one product or service that they are selling. I then explain that they are selling the same product or service that every other business in the world is selling. When all answers have finally been exhausted, I give them the real answer. With all attention on what I am about to say, I clearly tell them that the number one product being sold is trust. I then go on to explain that the only way that loyalty will ever occur is when our guests trust us enough to not only return, but also tell others about our great service. It is only when we have established trust that guest loyalty can occur.

It is only when we have established trust that guest loyalty can occur.

In order for us to win loyal guests, it is imperative that they trust us. The only way that we can establish this trust is to consistently provide them with outstanding service. When a Golf Club understands that guest confidence is the bedrock of every successful operation, then the goal becomes more focused. Instead of simply selling products or services, our focus now narrows down to establishing trust with our guests.

Instead of simply selling products or services, our focus now narrows down to establishing trust with our guests.

Without this, we will soon find guests looking for another place to patronize. This is because one of the main reasons that guests leave a Golf Club is because they have lost trust. Sometimes it happens because of one bad experience. If we are to build a great reputation, we must consistently give our guests great service that allows them to maintain solid confidence in us. This is because trust is the only reason that guests will ever want to return.

Who Are the Best People to Hire?

Every great guest service Golf Club is made up of a team of capable individuals who have certain innate qualities.

If we were to analyze a Golf Club that is known for providing outstanding service, we will soon recognize certain characteristics that each team member tends to have. These qualities give a clear advantage in consistently providing five-star service. What we will also find in these Golf Clubs is the ability to hire the best people for the position. This of course is the key in building great service. In the final analysis, great guest service is the result of having a great guest service team.

In the final analysis, great guest service is the result of having a great guest service team.

This is why the hiring process is so critical if we are to create a Golf Club with a reputation for outstanding service. Get the right people and great service will follow. The smart Golf Clubs look for certain qualities when they are deciding on whom to hire. These character traits give an indication of how well each potential employee will perform with guests. By understanding the following traits to look for when hiring, we will begin to make the right decisions in who is qualified in providing five-star service. Let's look at five character traits and see why they are important.

1. Hire those who are most interested in the job

When deciding what candidate would be best at delivering five-star service, it is important to recognize those who are most interested in the job. It sounds elementary, but this thought is widely overlooked in the hiring process. By basing part of our decision on how interested and eager each candidate is in obtaining the position, it can also give us a clear indication of how well the candidate will do in serving others.

Let's use an example. Candidate A comes to the interview and appears thrilled about the possibility of winning the position. Candidate B shows less enthusiasm and gives the impression that he is only slightly interested in the open position. With this information, what candidate would we want to serve our guests? Obviously we would pick Candidate A based on what we have observed. If both candidates were equally qualified, but Candidate A showed more enthusiasm for the available position, it should be an easy choice in who would win out. This enthusiasm will hopefully carry over in doing an excellent job. If we are to make the right decision in whom to hire, the first qualification that we need to focus on is finding out who really desires the position.

2. Hire those who have thankful attitudes

The attitude of thankfulness is essentially opposite to the attitude of complaining. If we are to produce five-star service, it is important to choose those who can convey appreciation to the guest.

If we are to produce five-star service, it is important to choose those who can convey appreciation to the guest.

One vital characteristic in all guest service superstars is their ability to show thankfulness to those around them. This attractive feature will draw guests back because everyone responds well to an attitude of gratitude. This is important to understand if we are to build a super guest service team. In order to find the most thankful candidates in the hiring process, we need to be aware of the attitude of each applicant. Are they thankful to have been given this opportunity to be interviewed? Do they project a grateful disposition? The more appreciation shown, the more likely the candidate will project this to the guest. By being aware of how appreciative each candidate is during the interviewing process, we can become more attentive of who may be the best person for the job.

3. Hire those who are "others centered"

Providing five-star service will only work when we have a team that is focused on others and enjoy meeting their needs. In order to do this it is essential that we hire those who have a heart to serve. The only way that this is possible is by taking our eyes off of ourselves and becoming others centered. In one of my earlier books I wrote on this subject and how important it is to stay away from what I had referred to as the *me, myself, and I syndrome*. This is where everything revolves around meeting my needs and my needs alone. The problem with this outlook is that it makes serving others difficult. When we have this selfish attitude we tend to provide poor service because our heart is not into meeting the needs of the guest. It becomes more of an inconvenience when a guest needs our assistance. A selfish attitude sees each guest as an interruption.

A selfish attitude sees each guest as an interruption.

It we are to hire the right people, it is vital that we get a sense of how much they enjoy helping others. We can hire service oriented people by asking the right questions and carefully listening to the answers provided. I would also go so far as to say that poor service is the result of being served by someone that does not have a heart to serve. This may be due to being struck with the *me, myself, and I syndrome*. The best service providers have the mindset that their job is about serving others. They arrive with the goal of servitude and have their eyes focused on others. They are the superstars of guest service.

4. Hire those who show enthusiasm

Enthusiastic people have a way of making the experience for the guest more exciting. Because we live in an economy where our guests want an experience along with the product, who is more qualified to offer this better than an enthusiastic person? How many times were you excited about purchasing a product or service and had the person assisting you enthused as well? They showed sincere enthusiasm and this only made your purchase all the more better!

They showed sincere enthusiasm and this only made your purchase all the more better!

This is the power of enthusiasm. On the other hand, how many times have you made a purchase and the person serving you showed no interest whatsoever?

Here is an example of how enthusiasm can make all the difference. Recently I took my wife and three children across the country on a train. We were going from Chicago to Grand Canyon and were very excited about the trip. Arriving at the station, we were not asked about our trip. In a sense we felt simply like a number waiting our turn to board the train. Once on the train, our trip to Arizona would take about a day and a half. In all of that time, not one employee inquired about our travels. Even though this did not dampen our enthusiasm, imagine how we would have felt if one of the train employees showed an interest and shared in our excitement. This alone would have made us perceive the service as excellent simply because someone took the time and inquired about our trip.

This alone would have made us perceive the service as outstanding simply because someone took the time and inquired about our trip.

If we are to produce great service, we need to surround ourselves with a team that actively takes an interest in each guest and share in their enthusiasm.

5. Hire those with a great work ethic

One final thought on hiring the right people who will deliver five-star service is to find those that are not afraid to work. By this I mean employing candidates with a strong work ethic. Excellent service is the result of having a team that can go the extra mile in meeting the needs of each guest. In order to do this, we need to hire those with a strong and solid work ethic. When a Golf Club is surrounded with people who know how to get the job done, we will find that five-star service soon follows.

How Do We Get Better?

Every Golf Club must continually look for ways to improve on their guest services in order to avoid becoming stagnant.

One of the major benefits of wanting to improve is that it helps us to avoid becoming sluggish and too familiar with the system. Only in wanting to better ourselves will we keep from becoming stagnant. When we have a desire to learn, we begin to take on a whole new dimension in the way we see life. Developing a desire to learn allows us to grow and move forward. This growth also gives us the advantage because of the improvements that follow. If we are to get better, it is imperative that we have this aspiration within us. This of course not only includes our service to others, but also our life outside of work as well.

I once read a quote that said the purpose of getting a college education is simply to create a mindset of wanting to keep learning. Having spent close to eight years at five different colleges and universities, I can attest that much of what I had learned in those years is long forgotten. But the one benefit that these years did give me was the desire to continue to learn. This is by far the real secret if we want to improve and become better both on and off the job. Let's now turn our attention to five quick tips for improving and getting better with our service to others.

1. We get better by regular training

One of the first avenues in becoming more efficient in guest service is by having regular training sessions. How frequent we train will depend on the level that we desire to obtain. The benefit of training courses is that it allows us to refocus our attention on the importance of providing great service. It becomes a refresher course in motivating our team to be aware of how well we are doing in serving others. Training also allows us to take away new thoughts and ideas that will improve our services, and in the end benefit the guest.

Training also allows us to take away new thoughts and ideas that will improve our services, and in the end benefit the guest.

The whole goal in attending seminars and workshops is to bring the service team back on track and renew the commitment in providing outstanding service. The knowledge gained will bring about positive changes and redirect our attention to the importance of giving excellent service to our guests.

2. We get better by asking for advice

Another sure way to improve in providing five-star service is not being afraid to ask for advice. *We must make the initiative.* This does not mean that we sit around and wait for others to offer us some great suggestions. If we are to become better, we need to pursue the counsel of others who may be able to give us some valuable insights.

If we are to become better, we need to pursue the counsel of others who may be able to give us some valuable insights.

The saying that two heads are better than one holds true, especially when it comes to building a better guest service team. The key here is to find those whom we respect and simply ask their opinion on whatever area that we may want to improve in. It may be our communication skills or the tone of voice that we project to others. If we sincerely want to improve in serving our guests, then asking others is the fastest way to get there.

Another important point to note is that most of our friends would be honored to offer their advice on a certain area that we are looking to improve on. Too often we do not ask for advice. To not seek the opinion of those we respect is like throwing away valuable information that was right at our fingertips.

To not seek the opinion of those we respect is like throwing away valuable information that was right at our fingertips.

I am convinced that asking questions and really listening would instantly help us to improve. As mentioned earlier, seek out the advice from those you admire and respect. We must also remember that there are many voices waiting to give their opinion. By being wise in who we listen to will make all the difference in receiving the right counsel.

3. We get better by saying yes more often

One way to rate a Golf Club on how well they perform guest service is by listening to how many times they say *yes* during the course of a day. Without question, the five-star operations have a way of telling their guests *yes* more often that telling them *no*. Let me observe a Golf Club and I will be able to pick up on how well they are with service simply by how many times they say *yes* to their guests. If I hear *yes* much more often than *no*, I can be sure that the Golf Club truly understands guest service. What I have learned over the years is that the superstars of guest service find a way to meet the needs of the guest.

What I have learned over the years is that the superstars of guest service find a way to meet the needs of the guest.

They will do whatever it takes to take care of their guests. On the other hand, I have witnessed where Golf Clubs were stuck in what I refer to as the *no syndrome*. It was as if they enjoyed saying the word *no* to their guests. If we truly want to become better at serving others, we need to find a way to say *yes* more often. Maybe it would take changing a policy or getting rid of the red tape that typically entangles guest service representatives *into being forced to say no*. It may be as simple as allowing those who work out in front the freedom to make choices that will benefit the guest. Whatever avenue is taken, make sure that it allows the guest to hear *yes* more often.

4. We get better by listening to the guest

The primary way that any Golf Club can improve in their overall guest service is by being open to listen. Guests by and far are our greatest resource because they are seeing from an outsider's perspective. We must never forget that our degree of service success is based on the guest's observation. In fact, it is the guest's perception that ultimately decides how well we do in the area of service.

It is the guest's perception that ultimately decides how well we do in the area of service.

In far too many cases, a Golf Club will rate their guest service based on how they perceive the service. In a typical scenario, a club will look at their guest service from the viewpoint of how they perceive it. This is a mistake because of the bias opinions that come into play. This is why it is vital to seek out the guest's perspective. They are in a perfect position to be more forthright in their opinions. We must never forget that what we may consider to be great service does not matter if it contradicts with the guest's perception.

We must never forget that what we may consider to be great service does not matter if it contradicts with the guest's perception.

They are the ultimate deciders on whether our doors will stay open or not. If we want to improve and obtain five-star status, it is vital that we find out how the guest views our service.

5. We get better by gleaning from others

I have saved what I consider the best for last. If we want to improve in the area of guest service, it is imperative that we learn from others. This means that we keep our eyes open when we are out in the marketplace. There are hundreds of excellent examples of how to give five-star service. Our job is to keep one eye open and closely observe how we are treated as a guest.

In my second book entitled *Customer Service Superstars*, I wrote the following:

"Every so often we are given the rare pleasure of being served by a guest service superstar. Not only have we been given excellent service, but we also walk away feeling valued and appreciated."

By keeping our eyes open and learning from others who offer great service, we will begin to improve ourselves. Those who understand how to give outstanding service always impress me. They have a way of showing themselves to be friendly and welcoming. This automatically increases my perception of the service. Over the years I have had the privilege of being served by these superstars and have learned that excellent service starts with projecting a great attitude. If we are to become better at serving others, remember to learn from those who are the experts in providing five-star service.

What Do the Best Golf Clubs Do Right?

The best Golf Clubs realize that people are the most important asset.

The winning operations understand the importance of human relationships and how this will ultimately decide how successful they are in the future. The heart of the matter is establishing healthy relationships. *How well we treat our guests will be the deciding factor in how we are judged with our service.* The moment that a Golf Club begins to fall will be the moment that they have forgotten what I call *the people factor.* Take care of people and you will take care of your Golf Club.

Another successful trait that the best Golf Clubs have is their drive to take care of both the guest and their own team. They never forget the importance of treating their employees fairly. If we were to take a closer look at the best Golf Clubs to work for, we would eventually discover their secret. This of course is that they understand the importance of taking care of their employees. They believe in the golden rule of management that states *"treat each employee the way you would like your employees to treat each guest."* Following are five areas that are consistently witnessed in the best Golf Clubs.

1. The best Golf Clubs hire the right people

Golf Clubs that do it right do so because they have the right people. Every great guest service Golf Club becomes this way as a result of having a group of individuals who work together in building a successful operation. In other words, the best Golf Clubs become this way because they have the best working team. They have a way of attracting and hiring the best qualified people. The process is done correctly and the personnel responsible have an innate ability to bring on board the best qualified at serving others. This is reflected in the service itself. Remember that successful Golf Clubs are a result of people, and if we are to succeed in delivering exceptional service, we must develop a great team that understands the importance of serving others.

2. The best Golf Clubs train their staff

As mentioned previously, the best operations take care of their employees. This includes keeping them motivated by providing them with periodical training programs that assist in keeping everyone on track. *When employees feel that the Golf Club cares about them, the employees in turn give their best.* There is an inner drive in each of us to perform at our highest level when we are motivated by someone who genuinely cares for our welfare. This motivation can come from the Golf Club or from an individual within the Golf Club. When training programs are offered, it subconsciously conveys to the employees that the Golf Club cares.

When training programs are offered, it subconsciously conveys to the employees that the Golf Club cares.

This can have a big impact on the overall performance. When we look at the advantage of offering programs for the employees, the benefits far outweigh the cost. As mentioned, the psychological impact of feeling the Golf Club cares will automatically improve the performance of the employees. It is also beneficial in that employees walk away with new information that will assist them in their quest to offer outstanding service.

3. The best Golf Clubs give more than expected

Nothing is more pleasing to a guest than being pleasantly surprised. One way to consistently offer this is to simply go the extra mile and give your guests the service that they were not expecting. In other words, surprise the guest by giving them great service. In reality this is not difficult to do since the majority of service in America is average. Understanding this will definitely work to your advantage. When we realize that most service is simply average, we will automatically surprise our guests when they see our service going the extra mile. This is what separates the best Golf Clubs from the others.

Think of it in this way. Our guests are not expecting much. They have had hundreds of experiences through the years with average to below average service. When they enter our doors, they basically expect the same run of the mill service. By simply showing ourselves to be more friendly and pleased to see them, we have automatically given our guests something that they were not expecting. We must remember this if we are to improve. Give a little more and your guests will walk away thinking that they had just experienced great service.

4. The best Golf Clubs listen to their guests

Earlier I spoke on the importance of listening to our guests. This is because they are the most important asset that any Golf Club has. Guests will tell us a lot about our service if we simply would have the courage to listen to their advice.

Guests will tell us a lot about our service if we simply would have the courage to listen to their advice.

The best Golf Clubs understand this and continually seek out the opinions of their guests. Without this input we will only be guessing at how well we are doing in the guest service department.

Listening to our guests fulfills two important roles in becoming our best. The first role of listening is that it tells the guest that we care about their opinion. This alone will have a profound effect in expressing to them that we care enough to listen to them. Another role of listening is that it actually can help us to improve our services without having to pay for it! It is free, unbiased advice coming from our most important source. If we are to improve and deliver five-star service, we need to copy the best Golf Clubs and seek out the opinions of our guests.

5. The best Golf Clubs respond quickly

One telling sign of a successful Golf Club is measuring how quickly they respond to their guests. This is especially true in the area of guest service over the telephone. The best Golf Clubs understand the importance of responding promptly. We need to give the impression that the guest's request is urgent and we will take care of it in a quick and efficient manner.

We need to give the impression that the guest's request is urgent and we will take care of it in a quick and efficient manner.

When guests take notice of our urgency to deliver them with their request, they in turn will automatically give us a higher rating on our service. Returning telephone calls promptly and getting back to the guest as soon as possible will leave them with a positive opinion of our service. In today's world, being respectful of our guest's time is the only way to go. Whether over the telephone or in person, we must consistently give the impression that the guest's time is important and we will do all that is in our power to take care of them. With this attitude we will not only deliver outstanding service, but we will also have our guests telling others about the great experience that they had.

Chapter 4
What Every Guest Appreciates
Understanding the Mind of the Guest...

The goal of this chapter will be to offer insights into how to exceed the expectations of the guest. My other goal is to explain the *seventeen essential needs* that must be met if we are to win their loyalty. By understanding these inner needs, we can then find ways to meet and exceed the guest's original expectations of our service.

Winning the guest will only happen when we consistently meet these seventeen needs. Every guest subconsciously is measuring our service based on whether or not we are meeting these needs. By understanding and then fulfilling these needs, we will eventually find more guests becoming loyal to our Golf Club.

If I had to summarize the most important key in winning the guest, it would be to gain their confidence. Once obtained, we can be sure that the service we are providing is also meeting another important need...which is to trust us.

#1 The Mind of the Guest...
Will make a decision within five minutes

The way to win guests in the first five minutes is to make them feel welcomed.

From the moment that a guest makes contact with a Golf Club, a decision on the overall service will be made within the first five minutes. Whether we realize it or not, every guest will unconsciously measure our service. If we start off great, the odds are in our favor that we will win their confidence. But if the service starts off on the wrong foot, more than likely we will not see them coming back.

Because of the many available options in today's world, the guest is offered a wide selection of similar Golf Clubs to choose from. This is why it is critical to win them from the start. This first impression will go a long way in deciding whether or not we will be seeing these guests in the future. These critical first few minutes are the most important timeframe for a new guest. They are in essence weighing whether or not they feel welcomed. If we give a great first impression, the guest will not only feel more secure in choosing us, but will also want to continue to return in the future. If this first impression gives them the confidence that they made the right choice in visiting our club, we will more than likely win them.

When a guest first enters a club, he or she is unsure about what kind of service they will receive. When we learn to graciously welcome them and provide a great first impression, it quickly dissolves any doubts and gives the guest the security he or she is looking for.

First impressions do matter. These first few minutes are critical in reassuring our guests that they have made a great choice in coming to us. How we perform during this initial introduction will stay with them for a long time.

The most important starting point is to offer each guest a friendly greeting and make them feel welcomed. Remember this tip and you will begin to win more guests to your side.

#2 The Mind of the Guest...
Is in a vulnerable position

The way to win your guests is to show them that you enjoy being accommodating.

Guests are essentially in a position of seeking assistance in either purchasing a product or service, or are simply looking for information. Because of this arrangement, they are put in a vulnerable position. In other words, the guest is asking for help, and this in turns creates a subtle sense of insecurity.

Think of it in this way. Most people function from day to day without a need for assistance. But once they take on the role of a guest, they are now in a position of asking for help. This can create an inner sense of uncertainty due to the fact that they are seeking assistance.

With this being the case, it would only be reasonable that we attempt to win their confidence by being as helpful as possible. If we consistently show ourselves to be supportive and accommodating, we will quickly win them.

In a high percentage of guest service scenarios, the guest simply feels like he or she is intruding. They feel like an interruption. This is why many refuse to ask for further assistance. The guest has been given the impression that he or she is bothering the service representative and has learned to stop seeking assistance.

If we are to win our guests, we must never project an impression that we are too busy or do not want to be interrupted. We must show through our facial gestures and actions that we are happy to help them.

Guests will offer high ratings on the service provided because we have made them feel that we were approachable. We need to give them the impression that we enjoy helping them. Without this, we will never win guest loyalty.

One further thought is to remember that our guests will only feel at ease when we convey that we are there to happily serve them. When we express to each guest that we are accommodating, he or she in turn will be more comfortable and willing to do business with us in the future.

#3 The Mind of the Guest...
Would like to be acknowledged

The way to win your guests is to acknowledge them with a friendly smile.

There is something powerful in acknowledging a guest through a friendly smile or a kind gesture. As mentioned in a previous chapter, it expresses that we are available to help them with any assistance that they may require. More importantly, offering a friendly sign of acknowledgement tells our guests that we have recognized them, and this in turn conveys a feeling of importance to them. What this also expresses is that we are happy and willing to lend a hand.

If we want to win guest loyalty, it is important to show that we are ready to help in a moment's notice. When we offer a friendly greeting, we are in essence telling guests that we are approachable and ready to assist.

What is Golfdifferent?

Golfdifferent is a new experience that will allow you to take a new look at golf. This is a different way of getting more excitement and fun into your golf course. It is simple, easy and last but not least a further source of income for your business.

Do you want to enjoy it? It can't be easier! You can choose among several possbilities. For instance by installing some fun spinners either at the tees or at the greens. Why not provide golfdifferent card games for purchase at your shop?

Card Games

Golfdifferent is a new, simple and fun card game! Players only have to take a card from the deck at the beginning of each hole. There the player will find either a forfeit for the player, a wild card or a challenge for an opponent. There is a wide variety of cards with hundreds of forfeits!

Spinners

Our Spinners are fun "wheels of fortune" that can be installed either on the output tees of the golf courses or on the greens (even in both!)
The player spins de wheel at the start of the pitch (or on arrival at the green) and follows the instructions given. There are boxes with either a favourable test, a test for an opponent or in the worst of cases a challenge for yourself. In addition to this, the spinner has a free space where you can put your own logo or even use it as a new a different marketing and advertising tool.

Spinners:
2 different designs available

Print your sponsor logo here

Golfdifferent **cards:**

Box: 350g C1S paper,
+ gloss lamination outside
each playinng box includes:
52cards, 8x8cm, 300g gloss paper

The cards are translated into
4 languages.

 English

 Español

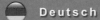 Deutsch

Français

Golfdifferent
email: info@golfdifferent.com
phone: 0034 988400078
Bajada al balneario 32 32459 Laias (Spain)

But what happens when a proper greeting is missing? What does this convey to our guests? The first thought that comes to mind is that a lack of acknowledgement expresses an unwelcoming feeling to the guest. He or she has taken the time to make contact with our Golf Club, and we have not properly recognized this.

When we do not show a friendly greeting, we are subconsciously telling them that we do not appreciate their business. It is as if we were saying that we really do not care that they have supported us.

The power of a warm welcome cannot be understated. It gives our guests a sense that we are happy to see them. It also tells them that we are user-friendly and available to assist at any time. More importantly, it expresses appreciation for choosing us.

Winning the guest is about treating them in an honorable manner. It is showing them that we care. Without an appropriate acknowledgement, we are telling our guest that he or she is not important. Simply remember that an appropriate greeting will suffice. As mentioned, it can be a friendly smile or gesture that will do the trick. Show a warm welcome and watch what happens.

#4 The Mind of the Guest...
Would like a sense of belonging

The way to win your guests is to create a sense of belonging.

When a guest enters through our door, he or she is measuring whether or not they feel accepted. This feeling of belonging will be a deciding factor in whether or not the guest will return in the future. With this said, it only stands to reason that we should create an atmosphere where our guests feel welcomed and accepted. When we show ourselves to be friendly and hospitable, it gives them the impression that they belong. It also gives a certain sense of security by being warmly received.

The feeling of belonging is a powerful attraction because of the measure of security that it brings to a person. We all like the feeling of being somewhere that gladly makes us feel welcomed.

In the art of serving others, we must never forget that every guest has a desire to belong. Without fulfilling this inner need, our chances of winning them will be close to zero. We may provide great service, but without giving the guest a sense of belonging, we will only be spinning our wheels. The best way to create a sense of belonging is by *becoming skillful in greeting people*. As mentioned in the previous chapter, a friendly welcome does not have to be elaborate or complex. It is simply showing ourselves to be pleasant and approachable.

Winning guest loyalty is about having the guest *want to return*. When we clearly understand this, we will begin to create a welcoming atmosphere that makes our guests feel accepted. We must be willing to go out of our way in order to make sure that their needs are being taken care of.

In the end, *great service is about creating an atmosphere that attracts guests*. It is about creating a feeling inside that gives them the desire to tell others about their excellent experience. Give each guest this sense of belonging and you will win them back.

#5 *The Mind of the Guest...*
Measures how friendly we are

The way to win your guests is to be friendly.

If we are to win our guests, it is essential that we are consistently showing ourselves to be friendly. Without this, we will never arrive at first base. Everyone is attracted to those who are genuinely cordial. We will always be ahead of our competition when we have what I like to refer to as *the friendly factor*. It draws people in and quickly dissolves any earlier defenses. Friendliness has a way of making others trust us because of the way we have treated them.

To win the guest, we need to do things that show that we are amiable. As mentioned earlier, this could include learning to smile more often. A simple smile is the surest way to offset any apprehensions that our guests may have when they first make contact with us. It quickly conveys that we are approachable and have a disposition that is good-natured. Another great way to show our guests that we are friendly is to express an interest in them. By taking an active interest in others, we are conveying that we care. It may be as simple as asking an appropriate question that then allows us to learn more about them. When we show that we are genuinely interested, it conveys a friendly attitude.

Winning guests can never happen if we have not learned the friendly factor formula. Loyalty will occur when we learn to build affable relationships. It begins with showing a friendly disposition and being genuinely interested in those whom we serve.

When all is said and done, our guests will judge our service by how friendly we were to them. They will measure this based on how we have made them feel. If we are to win them back, we must consistently show ourselves to be pleasant. Building relationships always begins by the simple act of friendliness. The proverb that states *"a man who has friends must show himself to be friendly"* holds true even in guest relationships. If we are to have loyal guests, we must show ourselves to be friendly as well.

#6 The Mind of the Guest...

Would like to be served...

The way to win your guests is to remember that they came to be served.

In order to win our guests, we must never forget that they would like to be served. It may sound elementary, but this simple fact is often forgotten in the guest service world. Guests enter with the desire to be taken care of. One of the allurements of taking on the role of a guest is the anticipation of being treated as a VIP. Of course in reality this seldom happens. But every so often we are offered excellent service and look forward to the next time we have the fortunate experience of being served by what I like to refer to as a *guest service superstar*. Guests enter with the hope of being served well. They secretly hope that our service to them will be first-rate. In their mind they desire to be taken care of that exceeds their original expectation.

But of course this rarely occurs. For many in the guest service field, their mindset is to take care of the guest in the easiest way possible. Instead of giving the guest an exceptional experience, many service representatives simply do minimal service without attempting to go the extra mile for the guest. It is because of these continual experiences that most guests do not anticipate that the service will be anything more than average. But deep inside they desire an experience that makes them feel like a VIP.

If we want to win our guests, we need to break out of just trying to get by with the service that we are providing and work toward giving our guests a great experience. We will create more loyalty because of the effort that is being put forth. We must remember that guests first and foremost enter our door to be served. They anticipate average service, but secretly desire to be served in a way that makes them feel like VIP's for a moment. If we can do this consistently, we will soon find ourselves winning more guests who will tell others about the exceptional treatment that they had received from us.

#7 The Mind of the Guest...
Measures how willing we are to serve

The way to win your guests is to be cheerfully willing to serve.

The superstars of guest service are noticed by their willingness to serve others. It is as if they feel honored to assist the guest. This trait alone is a major key in building a loyal following. The mind of the guest is not only measuring the service provided, but he or she is also weighing *our attitude and willingness to serve.* They are unconsciously gauging our enthusiasm to want to help. Our attitude in performing the service will ultimately become the determining factor in how others perceive our service.

Consider the moments that you have been assisted by someone who appeared to be reluctant to serve. How did that make you feel? Did you walk away sensing that the service was average or below average? More than likely what you had recognized was an unenthusiastic attitude that made the service less appealing. Now think of the times that you have received the best service. More than likely you encountered a service superstar who appeared to enjoy the act of assisting you. Their attitude made the service stand out. The reason for this is that guests ultimately measure the service by our attitude and willingness to serve.

Being willing to help others is essential if we are to win the guest. In my second book entitled *Customer Service Superstars*, I focused on the principal attitudes that make service superstars. In the end, the attitude that we have will be the determining factor in how our guests perceive our service. If our attitude is right, we will show it in the way we serve. Instead of viewing our duties as simply following a job description, we begin to see our responsibilities as an honor to help another person out. Not only will this perspective make our service stand out, but it will also draw guests back again. Remember that our willingness to serve is just as important as the service being provided.

Guests expect to get service but will be pleasantly surprised when we do it with a cheerful attitude.

#8 The Mind of the Guest...
Would like to be treated respectfully

The way to win your guests is to show proper respect.

If we are to win our guests, it is essential that we show proper respect. This is because conveying respect will consistently project that we appreciate their business. It also shows that we value them. Without appropriate regard for others, it becomes difficult to create great guest service. Every person is attracted to those who convey respect. This is one of the major reasons that respectful service representatives typically stand out above the crowd.

When all is said and done, our service will be measured by *the perception that the guest takes from the experience.* If he or she has not felt respected during their contact with us, they will more than likely rate our service as below average. On the other hand, when we consistently show a respectful attitude, our guests will perceive the service as above average. This is the power of respect. *It enhances the perception that the guest has of the service being provided.*

As mentioned earlier, showing respect expresses that we value others. If we are to win our guests, it is vital that we convey this *sense of significance* to them. When we offer the VIP treatment, we are in essence showing respect. We should always view our guests as important *simply because they are important.* Besides the fact that they are ultimately the ones who will decide whether our doors will stay open, our guests are fellow human beings. This fact alone becomes reason enough to honor them with respect.

Winning the guest has everything to do with making them feel worthwhile in having done business with us. It is having them walk away feeling that they were treated well and shown respect. When these two combinations are present, the goal of creating guest loyalty becomes more obtainable. Not only will they desire to return in the near future, but will not hesitate to tell others about us.

#9 The Mind of the Guest...
Measures how much we care

The way to win your guests is to have their best interest in mind.

Guests can quickly read how much we care by sensing if we have their best interest in mind. Without this, they will eventually look for another place to do business with. Caring is a sure way to win guest loyalty. This is because everyone is attracted to those who genuinely care. This attitude also builds trust and loyalty because our guests sense that we are looking out for them.

Is there a way to develop this quality that will make our guests notice something different in us? What is the key in becoming a more caring person? These questions can be answered in two words: *really care!* When we truly want the best for others, our whole outlook on life begins to change for the better. We start to treat others differently and become more thoughtful toward each guest. Without saying a word, our actions will show that we have their best interest in mind. Our guests will quickly pick up that we genuinely care that they are treated well.

So what does caring look like in the world of guest service? For one thing, the act of caring is shown in the way we focus attention on others. We recognize that our responsibility is to meet the needs of others. Instead of being self-centered, our life now becomes others-centered. Another way that we show concern is by going the extra mile in delivering excellent service. When our guests notice that we have gone out of our way in meeting their needs, they in turn will think more highly of our service. *It is the small things that will make all the difference in how the guest perceives our service.* If we are to win our guests, it is vital that we convey that we are looking out for them. It is showing that we care about their experience. When we do this, they will have a legitimate reason to tell others about our excellent service.

#10 The Mind of the Guest...
Would like help in making a decision

The way to win your guests is to assist them in making the right decision.

When we are serving guests, it is important to understand that they are anticipating our assistance. In many cases, the guest is undecided and is seeking our advice. We can help guide them simply by listening and asking the right questions. If we are to win the guest, it is essential that we learn how to lead them in making the right decision without appearing as if we are trying to push a quick sale. This is because nobody enjoys feeling as if they were being pressured. The key is to make suggestions that we feel would fit their immediate need and allow them to make the final decision.

There is a fine art in assisting a guest. We are to be there for them as well as be available to answer or offer suggestions. When we do this with professionalism, our guests will feel more confident in our suggestions. They will begin to trust that we are leading them in making the right choice. A large percentage of guests who make contact with a business are unsure about making a purchase. They may be undecided in whether or not to buy a product or service. In reality, many are looking for a knowledgeable person who will lead them with ideas and additional information.

The important point is to remember that we are to gather as much information from them in order to offer suggestions. As mentioned earlier, we are there to assist without appearing like salespeople simply trying to make a sale. When we ask the right questions and then allow the guest to make the choice, it then creates a certain amount of trust in the relationship. Our guests will not only appreciate that we have taken the time to listen, but they will also be won over by our professionalism. They will feel that we cared about their needs by the questions that were asked. They will also walk away with the feeling that we were very helpful. Find out what the needs of the guest are and simply direct them with the available choices that you offer.

#11 The Mind of the Guest...
Measures how knowledgeable we are

The way to win your guests is to be knowledgeable in the product or service being sold.

Guests expect us to be experts in the product or services that we provide. They enter with the expectation that we are knowledgeable and can direct them in making the right decision. In essence, they are putting their trust in the information that we provide for them. If we are to win our guests, it is vital to be educated in what we are offering. By being well-informed, we are giving them both the confidence and assurance that they will be directed in making the best available choice.

When a guest makes contact with us, he or she is in effect asking for assistance. They want us to be the experts in the product or services that are being offered. If the guest senses that we do not have sufficient knowledge, they will more than likely find another place to do business with. We must remember that every guest is seeking something in a service experience. In the majority of cases, this seeking is simply looking for answers. They ask questions in an attempt to not only find information about the product or service, but

123

also to test our knowledge. If we pass the test, the guest will then begin to put more confidence in the advice that is offered.

Winning the guest is about gaining their confidence. It is about having them trust the information that we are providing. Without having a high degree of knowledge, we can be sure that winning the guest will take place less frequently. It is only when we show a high level of knowledge and offer sound guidance that ultimately will win the loyalty of our guests. Reflect back on the times when you were playing the role of a guest and had inquired about a certain product. Looking back, it was those who showed a high degree of knowledge who eventually won your confidence. In the same way, our guests will gain more trust when we show ourselves to have a high level of knowledge in the product or service being offered.

#12 The Mind of the Guest...
Would like to be listened to

The way to win your guests is to listen and then ask the right questions.

Another sure way to win guests is by showing them that we are great listeners. Not only will they appreciate the fact that we have given them our full attention, but they will also feel that we genuinely cared about meeting their immediate needs.

Listening is a powerful communication tool. It conveys our interest in others and makes them appreciate that we have taken the time to clearly hear what they are saying. This is especially true with our guests. It expresses that we are there for them and attentive to their needs.

When the guest makes contact, he or she is in pursuit of information. They come with the goal of being provided with the best options available. By clearly listening to what their needs are, we are then in a better position to meet these needs.

Every guest would like to be listened to. He or she wants to feel that we have taken the time to really hear what they are inquiring about. One way to do this is to ask questions. When we listen and then ask a question back to the guest, it expresses that we are truly interested in what they have to say. It also tells them that we have heard them. If we are to win the guest, it is essential to understand what makes them want to return. One way to draw them back is to learn to listen more. As mentioned earlier, learning to pay attention and ask questions is a powerful tool to convey that we are good listeners.

Instead of telling guests what they need, it is better if we ask open ended questions that will allow them to draw up their own conclusions. *Open ended questions usually start with Who, What, When, Where, and How.* These types of questions will give the guest an opportunity to fully explain his or her needs. One final point is that listening also conveys that we are patient. When our guests sense this, they will appreciate the fact that we were more interested in their needs as opposed to simply following protocol.

#13 The Mind of the Guest...
Measures our manners

The way to win your guests is to show proper manners.

Great guest service is learning to exceed expectations. It is going above and beyond what the guest anticipated. To take the extra step and offer something unexpected will always give them the perception that our service was excellent. One way to do this is to always offer what I like to call *good old-fashioned manners.* Being a person who shows himself or herself to have pleasant manners wins every time. Even though it may be seldom noticed in the world of guest service does not mean that good manners have gone out of style.

The mind of the guest will be pleasantly surprised when we show ourselves to be polite. Everyone appreciates when another person is thoughtful toward them. Not only does it attract, but it also creates loyalty. When we talk about being a person of manners, we are mainly referring to our day to day conduct. In a sense, it is showing consideration and thoughtfulness. Simple phrases like *please* and *thank you* reflect pleasant manners.

Whenever we are looking out for the best interest in others, we are displaying good old-fashioned manners. Our guests will respond positively and be won over by the proper conduct that we have shown. Because genuine courtesy is seldom experienced in the marketplace, it is always refreshing for guests to be treated in such a way. Even though they may not say anything, we can be sure that our polite manners will eventually draw them back.

By going the extra mile and showing consideration, we are telling our guests that we not only value them as a person, but we also appreciate that they have patronized our club. And in the end, we will discover that these good old-fashioned manners really never go out of fashion.

#14 The Mind of the Guest...
Measures our efficiency

The way to win your guests is to respect their time.

One area in our service that will consistently be measured is our efficiency in providing excellent service in a timely fashion. Our guests will recognize when we have respected their time and rate our service higher simply because of this. Because we live in a fast-paced society, our guests would like to see that we serve them in a timely manner. Our goal is to show by our actions that we *respect their time* by being as professional and efficient as possible in our service to them. When they take notice that we are serving in a way that conveys to them that we respect their time, they cannot help but recognize our service as being excellent. This is because we are conveying to them that we recognize that their time is valued.

Winning the guest is about making the transaction as efficient as possible. In the mind of the guest, he or she is measuring how much we are respecting their personal time. If they perceive that we are taking our time, the message being conveyed is that we don't really care. In order to serve in an efficient manner, we need to fully understand our responsibilities to each guest. We also must understand how to conduct the transaction as quickly as possible. When we understand the total process involved in serving the guest, we will begin to offer better overall service.

Nothing can be more frustrating for a guest than to have to wait for a transaction that should have taken half the time. When this occurs, the mind of the guest makes a mental note not to return in the near future. In most cases, they will show their displeasure by simply not returning. Being efficient gives our guests the impression that we are professionals in our field of work. It tells them that we value their time and want to make their visit as pleasant as possible. Offer this and you will consistently win the guest.

#15 The Mind of the Guest...

Measures our consistency

The way to win your guests is to show the same consistency every time.

Every guest would like to know that our service will be consistent each time. They want to know that the great service they receive is going to be the same the next time they are doing business with us. Consistency also has a way of bringing security to our guests. Because our service maintains uniformity, it gives them the confidence that they will receive the same service in the future. When this happens, we can be sure that guests will want to return.

When our service is lacking in steadiness and stability, the guest then begins to view our Golf Club as unreliable. They feel that our service lacks any sense of direction and cannot be dependable. The result of this unpredictability is that the guest ends up looking elsewhere in an attempt to find more predictable service. The importance of dependable service cannot be understated. This is why a consistent and friendly attitude is so critical in the world of guest service. When we show ourselves to be reliable and steady, we give our guests the security that they are looking for when it comes to providing consistent service.

The mind of the guest wants to know that they will be treated exactly the same way each visit. They also want to know that the service is going to be the same every time. When this occurs, not only will they want to return, but they will also feel secure enough to tell others about the great experience that they have always received from our Golf Club. Loyalty takes place when guests have the inner security and confidence that we will not change. They do not like change, especially when the service offered previously was outstanding. In order to do this, we must make sure that everyone on our service team is consistently on the same page when it comes to service. It is only when our service maintains this consistent pattern year after year that our guests will eventually come to expect that we will take care of them in the same excellent manner.

#16 *The Mind of the Guest...*

Would like to be appreciated

The way to win your guests is to show that you appreciate their business.

One of the best gifts that we can offer our guests is to convey to them our sincere appreciation for doing business with us. This will make all the difference in whether or not we succeed with them. Not only will it attract more guests back, but it also satisfies the inner desire to be appreciated. When a guest visits our club, he or she has made the conscious decision to choose us over the competition. When we see it from this perspective, we in turn will begin to naturally show appreciation more often. This mindset of recognizing that every guest has other choices should make us all the more willing to show appreciation that they chose us.

Showing appreciation is a very powerful attitude. When it comes from a sincere heart, it attracts guests and gives them a reason to come back. We are in essence recognizing their true worth. This makes the guest feel valued to have patronized our club. On the other hand, if we forget to show that we appreciate their support, we are expressing that we do not recognize their value to our Golf Club. They walk away with an inner feeling that we do not recognize their worth.

Showing appreciation has a way of meeting the guest's internal desire to feel valued. They will appreciate the fact that we have recognized their worth and give our service higher ratings. This simple expression of gratefulness will not only win guests back, but it lets them know that we recognize their importance to the success of our Golf Club. In order to show gratitude, it is important that we express it from the heart. Our guests will be able to sense when we sincerely appreciate their business. They will be able to tell when we genuinely are thankful for their support. This will also give our guests a reason to return in the future and tell others about the service that was received.

#17 The Mind of the Guest...

Would like to trust us

The way to win your guests is to be a trustworthy person.

The ultimate goal in providing guest service is to build trust in our relationships with those we serve. *This is because winning a guest will never happen if trust has not been established.* From the start, the mind of the guest wants to know if we can be trusted. Their most important quest is to find out if they can put their confidence in our Golf Club. This will eventually be the deciding factor in whether or not loyalty occurs. It is paramount that we understand how to establish trust from the beginning if we are to win them to our club. As mentioned, the guest is seeking clues that will signify our trustworthiness. He or she may be measuring the way that we show respect and consideration. It may be in the way that we communicate either through our words or behavior.

When we show ourselves to be friendly and willing to help, our guests are more likely to trust us. *It really comes down to the little things that convey that we can be trusted.* By showing ourselves to be considerate and ready to lend a hand, we will quickly express that we are reliable in providing dependable service. Gaining this trust has many advantages when it comes to serving others. The biggest benefit is that our guests will not hesitate to tell others about us. They will gladly advertise our great service because of the trust that we have established with them. The confidence that they have in our ability will give them the assurance to tell their friends about us.

Without having credibility, the guest will more than likely find another Golf Club to patronize. This is why it is imperative to establish trust from the start. The first impressions that are made will be difficult to erase if we do not show our best from the onset. *Winning the guest is really about winning their trust.* It is about understanding their inner needs and doing our best to meet them. Be trustworthy and they will return.

Chapter 5
Picking the Right Service Team
The 5 Mindsets that Deliver Five-Star Service...

In every Golf Club that provides guest services, there is a certain level of service that will be expected. Depending on the type of facility and the anticipated expectations, each Golf Club must fulfill the guest's initial expectation if they are to be ultimately successful. Better yet, *if a Golf Club can exceed this anticipated service that the guest originally expected, he or she will walk away pleasantly surprised.* As mentioned, every guest will have a certain expectation level of the anticipated service prior to actually being engaged with the Golf Club. But what would happen if an establishment learned the secret of consistently exceeding the guest's expectations?

> *What would happen if an establishment learned the secret of consistently exceeding the guest's expectations?*

What if they consistently delivered exceptional service that even the most demanding guest had not expected?

There is a way to offer what I have termed *exceptional service* day in and day out. It will offer your guests exceptional service that even they had not expected. *This type of service can only happen with the five factors that I will be discussing in the following pages.* Any Golf Club can easily implement these factors if they will first understand that providing exceptional service must always begin with the correct frame of mind. It starts with having the right mindset.

131

Mindset #1
The Selfless Factor
"You're the reason I came to work."

From the moment we came into the world our natural inclination is to be self-centered. We arrive with the mindset of wanting to be served. This of course goes against the very first frame of mind that produces exceptional service, which is called the *Selfless Factor*. Let me offer a definition of what I consider to be the *Selfless Factor*:

"Developing the mindset that I came to the Golf Club today in order to serve."

If we are to offer exceptional service, the first goal is to get out of our own way and look to the needs of others.

If we are to offer exceptional service, the first goal is to get out of our own way and look to the needs of others.

The whole purpose of why we arrive at the club is to take care of the guest. It must not be about meeting our own personal needs. Providing exceptional service is about focusing more on our guests and their needs. Let's first look at where most guest services go wrong. In far too many Golf Clubs, the mindset is that those who serve are in charge.

In far too many Golf Clubs, the mindset is that those who serve are in charge.

They arrive with the wrong frame of mind. Instead of seeing their top responsibility as serving the guest, they arrive to work with the mindset that they are primarily there to meet their own needs. *The frame of mind for these service representatives makes it almost impossible to offer exceptional service because they are performing their duties with the focus on themselves.* Instead of showing up with the goal of serving others, they arrive with the mindset that they are there to meet their own needs. This of course is not to imply that trying to make a living is not important. Many who serve are motivated with the thought of having to earn a paycheck. But to solely allow this thinking to dominate the reason for working will make it almost next to impossible to consistently deliver exceptional service. This is because we are serving our guests from self-centeredness. In essence, our service becomes simply a means to make a living. With this frame of mind, we will find it difficult to offer exceptional service.

Consider the service that you and I encounter on a daily basis. If we look hard enough, we will discover that the majority of service performed is what I would refer to as *robotic service*. We get the impression that those who are responsible for serving are going through the motions of following a job description. We get the feeling that their heart is not in it. Of course there will be those special moments when we are served by what I like to refer to as a *guest service superstar*. These are the special service representatives who give us the impression that the only reason that they came to work was to provide us with great service.

Delivering exceptional service must start with creating the right frame of mind from the moment that we arrive in the parking lot.

Delivering exceptional service must start with creating the right frame of mind from the moment that we arrive in the parking lot.

We must develop the mindset that the reason we came to work is to serve the guests. Every other reason becomes secondary to this thought. As mentioned, we must realize that providing exceptional service can only occur when we are primarily focused on others. We must also understand that exceptional service will never happen when our interior motives are founded on selfish intentions.

Exceptional service will never happen when our interior motives are founded on selfish intentions.

This is because our heart will never truly be in it. When we *get out of the way* and serve with the sole purpose of the guest's best interest in mind, our service cannot help but reflect exceptional service. With self-centeredness taken out of the picture, our service now takes on a whole new perspective in that we arrive with the mindset to serve. As mentioned earlier, most service offered is not performed from a service-minded mentality. It is not delivered with the frame of mind of being a servant to others. In fact, to even suggest that a person's main responsibility is to be a servant may instantly bring resistance from those who typically perform average service at best.

To even suggest that a person's main responsibility is to be a servant may instantly bring resistance from those who typically perform average service at best.

This is why it is difficult for most in the service industry to reach their potential in the art of serving. They will not internally accept their primary role as a servant to others. Being thought of as a servant tends to make us feel uncomfortable. It goes against our nature. The word itself can make us think of being at the low end of the ladder. This is the reason that most service performed is considered average. *We simply may not accept this ideal that our main role is to serve.* This is also the reason that we fail in providing exceptional service. In order to understand the selfless factor, we must re-examine our inner definition of the word servant. This is because selfless service can never occur until we reconsider and begin to change our internal belief.

In reality, the duty of performing service essentially makes us a servant. The problem occurs when we reject the very thought that our role is to serve. Let me offer a few ideas that may give each of us a new perspective on the word servant. I am convinced that the absolute best service providers have no fears about taking on the role of being a servant.

The absolute best service providers have no fears about taking on the role of being a servant.

In fact, they welcome this without feeling as though they were being downgraded to a lower position. These are the people who may or may not understand that assisting others is where greater fulfillment in life takes place.

These are the people who may or may not understand that assisting others is where greater fulfillment in life takes place.

They have no problem with serving selflessly. This is because they are doing it with the motive that makes serving enjoyable. Their belief is such that service is about meeting another person's needs as opposed to simply doing it for self-centered reasons. This is why they consistently perform exceptional service.

Having this correct service mentality allows us to avoid serving with selfish motives.

Having this correct service mentality allows us to avoid serving with selfish motives.

We serve with the best intentions and gladly accept our position. *This is also why our service will consistently stand out.* When we joyfully take on the role of a servant, we begin to see serving from a new perspective. We have a new frame of mind and perform at a level that consistently exceeds the guest's expectations.

If I were to take a guess from both personal observation and discussions with others on the overall state of guest services, I would have to rate the average service at a *five* from a scale from *one to ten*. In a typical service scenario, most guests expect average service. *(In many cases they are inwardly hoping that the service will be at least average.)* The expectation of guests is somewhat average simply because they have been trained over the years to expect nothing more.

The expectation of guests is somewhat average simply because they have been trained over the years to expect nothing more.

135

As mentioned earlier, the reason for this average service is because service representatives arrive with the wrong frame of mind. *As mentioned, their reason for coming to work revolves around themselves.* They do not arrive with the mindset to serve. They perform their responsibility with little or no servant mentality. Many also arrive with the mindset that they are in charge and have every intention to do as little for the guest as possible.

Many also arrive with the mindset that they are in charge and have every intention to do as little for the guest as possible.

This *I'm in charge* mentality is the most detrimental attitude for providing exceptional service. This is where the guest walks in and immediately senses that he or she is intruding and feels unwelcomed. As guests, we are made to feel like an interruption and inwardly are just hoping to receive average service. When service representatives have this mentality, they will soon discover that fewer guests are returning. The reason for this occurrence is that these service representatives develop a detrimental attitude that they are in charge with little intention on serving others.

These service representatives develop a detrimental attitude that they are in charge with little intention on serving others.

They have a mindset that they have the power over their guests simply because they are behind the counter or in a position where the guest must rely on them. Having the mindset that they came to work with the sole purpose of serving is totally foreign to them.

I bring up this point to expose the leading detriment in providing exceptional service. As mentioned earlier in the chapter, exceptional service must begin with a frame of mind that is selfless. Arriving with the belief that we are there to serve is the only way that exceptional service can happen.

Arriving with the belief that we are there to serve is the only way that exceptional service can happen.

It is not about us and what we can get from it. It is gladly taking on the role of a servant and seeing our role as selflessly serving. The selfless factor is about learning to serve with the best intentions. It freely accepts the role of a servant without a fragile ego getting in the way. It is showing our guests that we are happily willing to assist them. When this occurs, we can be certain that we have taken a major first step in providing exceptional service.

Mindset #2

The Above and Beyond Factor
"I'll do whatever it takes."

Exceptional service is giving our guests what they would like. It is going above and beyond and offering them exceptional service. It is doing whatever it takes to meet the guest's request. It is serving with the attitude that a potential no becomes a positive yes. What the guest has requested becomes a reality. This second key to exceptional service is what I have coined the *Above and Beyond Factor*. It is taking the extra mile in providing excellent service to the guests. We not only are meeting their original expectations, but are exceeding them.

We not only are meeting their original expectations, but are exceeding them.

When this consistently occurs, we can be sure that we are performing exceptional service. As discussed in the previous chapter, one of the reasons that service is somewhat average is because those who are in the position of serving arrive with the wrong frame of mind. Instead of coming with a selfless mentality, these service representatives arrive to work unprepared to serve. They never truly understand that their duty is to take care of the guests. *In some cases, these ill-equipped service representatives view their position as a way of gaining a sense of power because the guest must now depend on their assistance.* Another reason that service is generally average is because very few want to go above and beyond the guest's original expectation. They look at their responsibility as simply meeting the guest's need with the least amount of energy. To consider going the extra mile in delivering exceptional service has seldom crossed their mind. In essence, these service representatives see their responsibility as nothing more than just getting by in the service being provided.

The reasons stated above are shared for one purpose: *to show the reader what must be avoided at all costs.* Our guests will recognize when we have an unmotivated attitude to serve. They will sense when we perform our responsibilities with the mindset that we are in charge and will only perform the least minimum service. Having this detrimental *"I'm the boss"* mentality will quickly lose guests in no time. Our guests will also recognize when we offer service that attempts to simply get by. They will feel that we did not attempt to offer them exceptional service. If anything, the guest will walk away feeling that we were trying to do the least amount of work in order to simply fulfill a job description.

If we are to offer exceptional service to our guests, we must learn to exceed their original expectations. We must discover what the guest's anticipated expectation is and surpass it.

We must discover what the guest's anticipated expectation is and surpass it.

This is what I refer to as the *Above and Beyond Factor.* In order to understand this concept, we must have a clear understanding of what the average expectations are of the guests. Depending on the type of facility, the typical guest will have a certain level of what will be expected. For example, a five-star Golf Club on a remote island will have higher expectations from the guests than a small local course in the middle of a small rural area. An exclusive Golf Club in a resort town will have higher expectations from the guests than a small facility in a small, Midwestern location. The point is that every establishment will have a certain level of service expectations.

Every establishment will have a certain level of service expectations.

In order to exceed our guest's expectations, we must have a clear picture of what they actually expect. Once established, we are now in a better position to go above and beyond and offer exceptional service. Once we understand this, it is now time to deliver. *Like every other factor that we will be discussing, going above and beyond must start with the correct mindset.* We need to develop the frame of mind that we will do whatever it takes to exceed the guest's expectations. This of course is where most Golf Clubs fall short in their service. They will only go so far in offering service to the guest. Instead of exceeding the expectations, most clubs simply attempt to get by and offer service that turns out to be average.

Most establishments simply attempt to get by and offer service that turns out to be average.

The roadblocks in providing above and beyond service are endless. It would take too long to give the reasons for this, but what I will do is expose *the top three reasons* that most establishments fail in exceeding the guest's expectations.

Reason 1: The wrong perspective on serving

At the top of the list of why most Golf Clubs fail to exceed the guest's expectation is that *they have a wrong view of serving.* Many in the service industry hold the belief that as long as the guest receives the service expected, they are doing a good job. The perspective held is that great service is simply meeting the guest's needs.

The perspective held is that great service is simply meeting the guest's needs.

139

But what they do not realize is that the majority of guests walk away feeling that the service performed was average or below average. If we are to offer exceptional service, it is vital that our perspective on what constitutes exceptional service change.

If we are to offer exceptional service, it is vital that our perspective on what constitutes exceptional service change.

We cannot look at serving as simply meeting our guest's needs. It must go beyond this. The reason for attempting to go above and beyond is that our guests expect us to meet their needs. *It will come as no surprise to them when we do what is expected.* This is why most guests walk away unimpressed with the service that they were provided.

Exceptional service is finding a way to go above and beyond what our guests expect. To simply meet their request is considered average service in the eyes of the guest.

To simply meet their request is considered average service in the eyes of the guest.

If we want to exceed their expectations and offer exceptional service, we must change our thinking on what truly defines exceptional service. We must clearly understand that if we give our guests what they had originally expected from us, they will continue to rate our service as average. But when we begin to redefine and develop a new outlook on what constitutes exceptional service, our service will move to a higher level and become instantly noticeable to those we serve. All it takes is learning to offer more than what was expected.

All it takes is learning to offer more than what was expected.

Reason 2: The chains of policies and rules

The second reason that most clubs fail in providing exceptional service is because of the policies and rules that are set in place to discourage exceptional service. Without realizing it, these policies end up benefiting the Golf Club more than the guests.

Without realizing it, these policies end up benefiting the Golf Club more than the guests.

Not only do they restrict the service representatives from being able to deliver exceptional service, but they also leave the guests with an experience that is soon forgotten. It happens all the time. *Golf Clubs implement a policy or rule with no thought of how this will affect the service being provided for the guests.* Without realizing it, what they have done is create a policy that restricts the service representatives from offering the guest exceptional service.

This is not to say that setting policies and rules at an establishment is wrong in itself. But what I have found over the years is that the vast majority of these regulations limit the possibility of ever delivering exceptional service. What needs to take place is to re-examine the rules and see if they are really necessary. More importantly, every policy should be looked at from the guest's point of view.

Every policy should be looked at from the guest's point of view.

Will this benefit the guests or be a stumbling block in offering them the best possible service? When it becomes unclear on whether or not the new policy will benefit guest services, then it may be a red flag and should be removed as quickly as possible. We must remember that if exceptional service is to take place at our facility, we must allow our guests as much freedom as possible in being able to enjoy the overall experience that we are trying to create for them. Do whatever it takes to allow this and you will find exceptional service occurring.

Reason 3: Never asking for opinions

The final reason that most Golf Clubs fail to offer exceptional service is because they are blindly trapped in believing that their performance with the guests is excellent. Even though they have never sought to inquire about the service from those they serve, these clubs live in a sheltered cocoon by accepting only their own opinion.

If I were to visit fifty Golf Clubs and asked them how they would rate their service from one to ten, the average rating would be somewhere around an eight. *If I were then to ask if they periodically do surveys with their guests on the service that they offer, the vast majority would answer no.* In other words, these Golf Clubs are giving their service high marks with no idea what their guests think.

These Golf Clubs are giving their service high marks with no idea what the guests think.

How can we honestly receive a true reading of how well we are doing if we ignore how the guest feels about our service? *It becomes one-sided in that we disregard and overlook the opinion that matters the most.* Does it really matter what we think of our service if it does not match the guest's opinion?

Does it really matter what we think of our service if it does not match the guest's opinion?

In fact, I am convinced that service will always take a downturn when we begin to ignore the opinions of our guests. Going above and beyond what the guests expect is really about discovering what their expectations are in the first place. If we choose to ignore what they think, we have lost an invaluable *(and free)* resource for improving our service. Our guests have the advantage in that they see our service from another vantage point. They come with no predisposition or favoritism. If we can simply find out how they perceive our service, we will instantly begin to improve.

Going above and beyond is having the freedom to turn a no into a yes. It is doing whatever it takes to exceed the guest's original expectations. Instead of looking at service as simply meeting the guest's needs, *we need to see it as going beyond what he or she had originally expected.* Exceptional service is also being free from any restrictions that would get in the way of exceeding these expectations.

Mindset #3

The Care Factor
"I want your visit to be exceptional."

When serving, there is an unspoken message that is consistently being projected to our guests. Without a word spoken, our mannerisms and actions convey this important message. *The message that is being expressed* is *how much we really care.* Of all the subliminal clues that are being measured by our guests, none is as powerful as how much they perceive that we care about their overall experience at our club.

Of all the subliminal clues that are being measured by our guests, none is as powerful as how much they perceive that we care about their overall experience at our club.

I consider this factor to be *the heartbeat of exceptional service.* I also believe that many facilities overlook this most important aspect in providing exceptional service. *Our guests expect us to serve them. They expect us to be proficient and professional. What they may not expect is that we genuinely care that they are well taken care of.* The power of caring *is* the strongest ingredient in delivering exceptional service.

The power of caring is the strongest ingredient in delivering exceptional service.

143

Our guests cannot help but be pleasantly surprised when we genuinely care that they are well taken care of. *This thought is almost a foreign concept in the service training programs provided by many clubs.* So how can we define this caring factor without sounding to sentimental? Is there a way to describe it that will be understood and implemented by our staff members? *I believe that if we can see caring from a logical point of view, we then will be able to come to a consensus that caring should be a major part in service training.* If I had to define caring in the arena of serving the guests, my first thought would be that I would want to treat them in a way that would be desirable if I were the guest. *In other words, I would want to treat them the way that I would want to be treated.* By playing the role of a guest, I would want to be treated in such a way that conveyed to me that the staff was looking out for my best interest. I would want him or her to treat me with consideration. In other words, I would want to feel as though the server genuinely cared about me. Those who are best in serving have a genuine concern for their guests.

Those who are best in serving have a genuine concern for their guests.

This is one of the reasons that they gather guests who are fiercely loyal to them. The superstars of service consistently project an attitude that conveys their genuine concern for each and every guest. *What they understand is that loyalty occurs when genuine care is at the center of service.* Being able to offer exceptional service would be difficult if caring were not involved. This is because guests are measuring how concerned we are that they receive exceptional service. More importantly, they want to trust us enough to tell others about their great experience. But this will never occur unless the guest senses that we first and foremost care about their experience.

When a guest reflects back on the service received, his or her measurement is based primarily on the experience. The decision made about the service provided is based primarily on how they were made to feel throughout the experience.

The decision made about the service provided is based primarily on how they were made to feel throughout the experience.

By understanding that the guest's perception of the overall service is determined *by a feeling* is an important concept to be aware of. In the majority of cases, the guest will make a final decision on the service performed based on how they were made to feel. If this is the case, then it only goes to reason that having a genuine concern for how well the guest is served is critical if exceptional service is to be obtained. Since our guests are measuring our service primarily on how they felt during the experience, we must convey by our actions that we sincerely care that they are treated well.

Since our guests are measuring our service primarily on how they felt during the experience, we must convey by our actions that we sincerely care that they are treated well.

This alone can have a profound effect on the final outcome of how our service is perceived. Any Golf Club can improve in serving their guests if they begin to understand the power of caring. Not only will the service be perceived as exceptional, but the guests will be pleasantly surprised that those serving them had a genuine concern that their experience was excellent. This now leads to the question of how to improve in this area. Is there a secret in communicating to those we serve that we genuinely care that they receive the best possible service? What is the best way to show our guests that we are looking out for their best interest? My answer to these questions is that unless we honestly care, we will never reach our potential in the area of exceptional service.

Unless we honestly care, we will never reach our potential in the area of exceptional service.

Without a genuine concern, our service will be viewed as average. But when we serve with a caring attitude, our service begins to reach a new level that will be recognized by those we serve.

When we lack a genuine concern, our service is looked at as simply going through the motions of following a job description. Providing exceptional service is next to impossible because our heart is not genuinely in it. Our guests will sense this and go away with the feeling that there was something missing in the service received. If we were to reflect on the various services that we have received in the past, *we will discover that most gave us the impression that it was performed more out of obligation.* We get the sense that those who had assisted us were simply following a job description with little thought of how we were feeling during the experience. But then there were those *five-star moments* when we have been assisted by someone who made us feel as if he or she genuinely cared that we were given exceptional service. More than likely these service superstars had a way of treating us that conveyed their sincere desire to make our experience extraordinary. What they were performing was exceptional service. *We walked away with a feeling that they had our best interest in mind.*

I believe one of the main reasons that the caring factor is not more highly promoted in the world of service is because it has not been recognized for what it can truly do for the guest. Most guest service training focuses more on following a set pattern of procedures with little thought on the emotional side of serving the guest.

Most guest service training focuses more on following a set pattern of procedures with little thought on the emotional side of serving the guest.

Instead of viewing service as creating an experience for our guests, the vast majority of training focuses on policy manuals and responsibilities. *What is missing is focusing on the importance of meeting the guest's emotional needs.* We must remember that the guest's emotional experience is the determining factor in how he or she will rate our service.

The guest's emotional experience is the determining factor in how he or she will rate our service.

Exceptional service can be said to be both physically and emotionally meeting the guest's needs. This is why the caring factor makes all the difference in how the guest will perceive the experience. Not only have we met the expectations of being physically served, but the guest becomes pleasantly surprised when we convey that we sincerely care that their experience was exceptional. The way to express that we care is to give our guests the best service possible. It is showing that we genuinely would like their experience to be extraordinary. Not only will our service be perceived as first class, but our guests will walk away with the desire to tell others. This will happen when we serve with a heart that genuinely cares.

Mindset #4

The Honored Factor
"I feel privileged to serve you."

Of all five factors, I would consider the *Honored Factor* to be the attitude that separates the elite from the rest in the service industry. This factor is obtained by a very small percentage that has come to understand how this attitude positively enhances the overall experience for the guest. The *Honored Factor* is the ticket that automatically ushers a person into the *World Hall of Fame for Service Representatives.*

The Honored Factor is the ticket that automatically ushers a person into the World Hall of Fame for Service Representatives.

The reason that this factor is the rarest of all factors is simply because it is difficult for most people in the guest service industry to comprehend. I would go so far as to say that the vast majority of people have never even had this thought cross their mind. Unlike the other four factors, developing an attitude of feeling honored to serve is a totally foreign concept for most people to comprehend. If there were a way of selecting the top service superstars in the world, I would venture to say that this attitude is prevalent in each of them. Not only do they feel honored to serve their guests, but their actions show it time and again. Guests automatically sense right away that they are being served by someone who makes them feel like a VIP.

Before we continue to explain the benefits of seeing serving as a privilege that also should be enjoyed, we will look at what I consider to be the definition of honoring others during the act of service. Once understood, I believe we can then understand why this factor is essential if we are to reach a new level in our service. To honor another person is exactly what it says. We show others by our attitude and actions that we feel privileged to serve them.

To honor another person is exactly what it says. We show others by our attitude and actions that we feel privileged to serve them.

We look at our guests as if they were the most important person in the world at that moment. It would be similar to the attitude that we would capture if the President of the United States were to join us for dinner in our home. Not only would we want the visit to be as pleasant as possible, but we would feel honored to have the privilege of serving this important person. With this mindset, our service would more than likely be outstanding. We would make sure that the President would be well taken care of and provided with exceptional service. Now imagine if we were to treat every guest in the same manner that we had treated the President of the United States. Imagine how the guest would feel as he or she sensed that we were privileged with the opportunity to serve them. More than likely they would feel like the service provided made them feel like royalty. Exceptional service is about giving our guests the feeling of importance.

Exceptional service is about giving our guests the feeling of importance.

It is letting them know by our attitude that we are honored to serve them. It is doing our absolute best to accommodate them and make their experience memorable. When we truly grasp the importance of treating others with honor, we have taken the first step in understanding this powerful factor. *A good question that we can ask in determining how close a service representative is in capturing the honored factor is to find out how important he or she feels their guests are.* This answer alone will provide us with an accurate picture of whether or not they are qualified to offer exceptional service. If a person has never considered this question, then maybe it is time to stop and begin to understand the importance of each and every guest. When we truly value others, our tendency will be to treat them well.

When we truly value others, our tendency will be to treat them well.

By recognizing each guest's significance and worth, our service toward them will begin to take on new meaning. We will start to look at serving as an honor and a privilege. This mindset will not only produce exceptional service, but it will also change the way we conduct ourselves toward others. I have come to recognize that those who are best at offering exceptional service do so because of the way they view their guests. Instead of assisting others simply out of obligation, these service superstars appear to see serving as a privilege. This is because they view each person that they serve as someone to be honored.

Instead of assisting others simply out of obligation, these service superstars appear to see serving as a privilege. This is because they view each person that they serve as someone to be honored.

This is one of the major reasons that their guests walk away feeling as if they were given the VIP treatment. The service received made these guests feel important. *This feeling was real because the person serving them genuinely believed that they were important.* How we treat our guests essentially is a reflection of how valuable we perceive them to be.

How we treat our guests essentially is a reflection of how valuable we perceive them to be.

If we look at those we serve with little regard, it will show in the way that we have treated them. But if we see each guest as someone who is valued, it will show in the way that we conduct ourselves toward them. This can be seen in the example of the President of the United States. We would treat this guest with honor and respect. We would also feel privileged to be able to have the opportunity to serve. In similar fashion, if we can learn to treat everyone that we serve in the same manner, our service would automatically be outstanding. It is changing our view of others that will produce exceptional service.

It is changing our view of others that will produce exceptional service.

Imagine going to an upscale restaurant and being treated as if you were the most important person in the world. The service was conducted in such a manner that made you feel valued. Everything from how you were treated to the way that you were spoken to gave the impression that they felt privileged to serve you. Because of this, you wanted to tell others about the excellent experience.

The reason that the *Honored Factor* is seldom experienced in the service industry is because it is rarely taught and understood.

The reason that the Honored Factor is seldom experienced in the service industry is because it is rarely taught and understood.

The misunderstanding comes because few recognize the importance in how we view the guest. In a vast majority of cases, the service is conducted from the standpoint of following a list of steps and procedures. *The real problem comes by not teaching on the importance of how we perceive our guest's real value as a person.*

I am convinced that if service training would emphasize learning to honor others more, the service would immediately improve. Emphasize the importance of each guest and the serving would take on a whole new meaning. *It is the perception that needs to change.* When our training is focused on the fact that each guest is first and foremost a human being that deserves to be honored, our serving will begin to change for the better. Each guest will then be looked upon as a VIP deserving VIP treatment. We could almost say it would be like seeing each guest as the President of the United States!

Earlier I mentioned that serving others with honor will take place when we change our perception. In other words, how well we serve can ultimately be measured by how much value we give to others. Our outlook will be the decisive factor in how well we do. Similar to the *Caring Factor*, the *Honored Factor* really comes down to how much value we place on others. Where most service only appears like someone following a job description, *exceptional service is going beyond the surface in that it is bestowing value and honor on the guest.* When we give our guests a sense that they are valued, they in turn respond better. *By showing them honor, we are also conveying our sense of feeling privileged in having the opportunity to serve them.* I cannot stress this last point enough. When our guests sense that we feel honored and privileged to serve them, they look at our service as outstanding.

When our guests sense that we feel honored and privileged to serve them, they look at our service as outstanding.

As mentioned, this level of service rarely occurs in the real world. In far too many cases, the guest either feels like an interruption or senses that the server is simply following protocol. Instead of feeling valued, the guest walks away feeling like a number in a line. But by learning to change our perception and viewpoint of the value of each guest, our service will take on a whole new dimension.

By learning to change our perception and viewpoint of the value of each guest, our service will take on a whole new dimension.

We will treat people differently. We will be more respectful. Our tone of voice will be more pleasant, and our willingness to serve will change for the better. In the end, it really comes down to how valuable we see others.

Mindset #5
The Appreciation Factor
"I appreciate you."

As we approach the final factor that will consistently produce exceptional service, I am confident that this key will unlock the potential in every person. This final mindset is called the *Appreciation Factor*. By understanding how this will totally change your service toward others, you will also begin to notice your life changing as well. The *Appreciation Factor* is an attitude that makes us view life differently. As someone who serves others, our guests will instantly see a difference in the way we conduct ourselves toward them. This is the power of appreciation. I like to see this attitude as an inside change manifesting itself outwardly. Our disposition toward life begins to take on a whole new meaning because of the way that we are more appreciative. Instead of grumbling and seeing situations as gloomy, our thankful attitude overcomes every obstruction. This is especially true when it comes to providing exceptional service.

Before showing what appreciation does to our guests, let me define it from a service point of view:

"Appreciation allows us to serve with a more attractive attitude that conveys to others our joy in being able to serve."

There is something different when we are in the presence of a person who appreciates life. Not only do we sense that he or she has something that is desirable, but we somehow recognize the positive attributes in being a thankful person. Now imagine being served by a person who lives with this grateful disposition. Not only do we immediately recognize his or her positive outlook on life, but we are also impressed with their exceptional service toward us.

Assisting others with a lifestyle of appreciation is the best factor for changing our attitude toward serving. No other mindset can bring about changes quite as powerful as appreciation. *If we are to produce exceptional service, it is important to do it with the right mindset.* This is because our guests will foremost be measuring our attitude and willingness to serve. When we have a disposition of being a thankful person, our guests cannot help but see our service as superb.

> *When we have a disposition of being a thankful person, our guests cannot help but see our service as superb.*

Being thankful toward others also delivers the feeling of value. Similar to the *Honored Factor*, showing others our appreciation makes them feel like VIP's. It conveys our sincere appreciation that they have supported our establishment. This is vital because of the many options available in today's world. When we show our sincere appreciation, our guests will feel good that they have decided to patronize our Golf Club.

Every human being desires to be appreciated. They crave the sense of feeling that another person has recognized their true value.

> *Every person desires to be appreciated. They crave the sense of feeling that another person has recognized their true value.*

This is all the more true with our guests. They desire to be appreciated. They also would like to sense that we are grateful for their support. Without this, the guest walks away sensing less valued and appreciated. Those who consistently deliver exceptional service recognize the importance of showing others gratitude. They also recognize the significance of meeting this inward need of each guest. Visit a Golf Club that consistently delivers exceptional service and we will notice their show of appreciation. Not only have they offered exceptional service and exceeded the guest's expectations, but they also have met the guest's inner need to feel appreciated.

When we build a team that understands the importance of appreciation, we will begin to watch as our service improves. I will go so far as to say that the premiere Golf Club service teams consistently show their guests appreciation.

The premiere Golf Club service teams consistently show their guests appreciation.

I believe that one of the reasons that many clubs never obtain this final factor is because they do not understand the importance of showing gratitude toward others. Instead of training their team to meet this inward desire of the guest, the typical Golf Club simply serve without getting below the surface to the guest's inner emotional needs. The service becomes what the guest expected. Even the tone of voice in telling the guest thank you appears to be generic. If more Golf Clubs would implement into their service training the importance of conveying to the guest a deep sense of appreciation, the overall perception of the service would automatically improve.

If more Golf Clubs would implement into their service training the importance of conveying to the guest a deep sense of appreciation, the overall perception of the service would automatically improve.

Expressing appreciation goes much farther than simply saying thank you. To say thank you without genuinely meaning it does little for the guest. *It must come from the heart.* It must show itself in not only our mannerism and service, but also with a positive attitude. If it is not real, the guest will walk away with an inward sense that we did not truly appreciate his or her business.

Exceptional service is about creating a feeling for our guests. It is a perception that they walk away with.

Exceptional service is about creating a feeling for our guests. It is a perception that they walk away with.

Most expect to be served. What most guests do not expect is to have their longing to be appreciated met. The only people qualified to meet this need are those who are sincere and have an attitude of gratitude. If we are to truly touch another person with a sense of appreciation, we must serve *(and live)* with a thankful heart. Anything less will simply not do. When we live with this appreciative mindset, our service will instantly improve as well. We will go about with an attitude that projects that we are happy to assist others. Our guests will see our service more positively because of our willingness to serve.

Our guests will see our service more positively because of our willingness to serve.

Being appreciative will also assist in creating an atmosphere that makes the guests feel more welcomed. They sense our appreciative outlook and instantly feel more relaxed and comfortable.

Finally, serving with appreciation allows us to be more approachable to our guests.

Serving with appreciation allows us to be more approachable to our guests.

They will sense our friendliness and be more confident in telling others about the service that we have provided. In the end, having the

Appreciation Factor is a win-win situation for not only delivering exceptional service, but also for living a more fulfilled life.

If we are to offer this exceptional service on a consistent basis, our goal is to learn to serve with these five mindsets. As we begin to see serving with a new frame of mind, we will also start to see changes in the way that we treat our guests. *Instead of looking at our service as simply following a job description, we will begin to view it as a way to assist in making another person's life better.* By assisting others to our best ability, we will take on a new perspective in seeing that we are making a positive difference in the world. Not only are we offering exceptional service, but we are also bringing out the best in ourselves. *This is the ultimate benefit of being a willing servant toward others.*

As we come to a close in this chapter, my sincere desire is that each reader will take on a new outlook in the area of service. May we see that our greatest moments in life are a direct result of serving others. May we also discover that serving others is one of the best ways that we can begin to live with greater purpose and fulfillment. Remember these five factors and your team will begin to offer your guests exceptional service.

Chapter 6
It Comes Down to People Skills
9 Qualities That Enhance Serving Others...

What is it that allows some people to consistently offer excellent service while others struggle in their quest to deliver outstanding service? Why are some people better in their ability to serve than others? What qualities are needed to build a better service team? These are great questions that we will be addressing in the final chapter. My goal is to clearly show that building better Golf Club services and improving on our people skills is a direct result of developing more qualities into our own lives. In other words,

Better service correlates with the number of inner qualities that we have developed in our own lives.

If we are to build better guest services, the first and most important area that we will need to focus on *is ourselves.* It must start with taking an accurate and intimate look into our own lives and count how many qualities that we possess, and how many are missing. When we do this, we will begin to discover that the qualities that are missing *may be the reason that we are lacking in delivering excellent guest services.*

If we are to improve, we must understand that the qualities within essentially will determine how we treat others. For instance, if we are impatient with guests, we will tend to treat them in a manner that reflects annoyance. On the other hand, if we have developed the quality of patience, we will find that our treatment toward others

157

immediately improving. Not only will we be more understanding, but we will also be more considerate in our conduct.

Having excellent service skills is nothing more than treating others in a manner that we would like to be treated ourselves. *The excellent service teams bring out the best in others because they consistently are showing the following nine qualities that we will be briefly discussing.* If we are to improve and become better at guest services, we must first examine ourselves and learn how to develop more of these qualities into our lives.

When all is said and done, most of what will be shared is simple common sense. These nine qualities are nothing new. As a matter of fact, they have been around for centuries and have worked in every generation. It does not matter what part of the world we may visit or the culture involved. Every person will recognize these inner qualities as good character traits. *All it takes is to start with one quality and build from there.* Before long we will find that each new quality that is gained will begin to enhance not only our Golf Club services, but also our very lives. Even though some of these qualities have been discussed in earlier chapters, their role in providing outstanding service cannot be understated. Let's now take a look at these nine qualities essential for helping us to deliver exceptional service to the guests who visit our club.

Quality #1
Appreciation

It has been said that one of man's greatest desires is to be appreciated. This is because we feel valued when another person has recognized us. Appreciation is accepted universally and is a virtue that gives another person a sense of worth.

If we are to become our best, it is essential that we learn to show others that we appreciate them. Maybe it is something they did or said. Maybe it is something about their personality that we find likable. *Whatever it is, the important point is to let others know that we appreciate them.* It can be as informative as expressing a kind word or writing an appreciative letter to the person.

By expressing appreciation, we also are showing others a quality that they may not have recognized in themselves. We are essentially helping this person by recognizing something that can bring out certain gifts that he or she may not have been aware of. Remember to show sincere appreciation both on and off the job and watch as your people skills begin to improve considerably.

Quality #2
Cheerfulness

We often remember when we have encountered a person with a cheerful disposition. Not only did it awaken us, *but it also had the tendency to make us feel cheerful as well.* Having good people skills is about being able to create an atmosphere of optimism. It is drawing out the positive features in others and helping them to be more optimistic in the process.

Showing cheerfulness can be defined as a virtue that sees life from a more positive point of view. It is seeing the goodness in situations and meditating on things that are of quality. It is being a person who sees the best in others. When we have this type of attitude, we will find our service to others instantly improving.

If we are to have healthier relationships in our service to others, we need to look at life with a more joyful frame of mind. *By being aware of what we meditate on, we will begin to catch ourselves when our thoughts begin to become cloudy.* Start by seeing the goodness in life and the blessings that are given each day. When we do this, we will find ourselves becoming more cheerful with our guests, better at serving others, and improving on our relationships.

Quality #3
Dependability

Everyone enjoys being around those who are dependable. Not only are they trustworthy, but they can also be relied upon to do what they have said they would do. When others recognize this trait in us, it gives them the confidence that we can be depended upon. *This quality brings out the best in everyone simply because it creates a sense of trust.*

Having excellent people skills means that we project a life of dependability. It is putting an inner quality into action that allows people to trust us. When we are a dependable person who follows through on our commitments, we are also showing that we can be trusted with consistency in our service.

Words like reliability, consistency, and responsibility come to mind when we show that we can be depended upon. It gives others on our team a great example to follow. *The more dependable we are, the more we will find both our relationships and Golf Club services improving for the better.*

Quality #4
Friendliness

When people meet each other, the very first measuring tool being used is based on the feeling of friendliness. I like to call it the *friendly factor*. They make their first judgment based primarily on how friendly the other person was to them. This first impression is a major factor in how the relationship will progress in the future.

Developing excellent people skills and guest service is having the ability to project to others that we are good-natured. One clear way to do this is by showing ourselves to be friendly. *The foundation for any healthy relationship must begin with this virtue. It is the quality that gives our guests the green light that we are approachable.* Without this initial impression, it becomes difficult to develop great service at our Golf Club.

Being friendly is nothing more than showing ourselves to be considerate and pleasant toward others. It is being accepting and welcoming at the same time. *This is at the heart of great people skills.* It is making our guests feel comfortable from the start by our friendly disposition. *If we are to have guest loyalty at our club, we must always remember to show ourselves to be friendly.*

Quality #5
Goodwill

When we want the best for others, we are essentially showing goodwill toward them. The essence of goodwill is creating an atmosphere of unity where people encourage and bring out the best in each other. *Not only is this quality the foundation for building healthier relationships, but it is also the key for developing outstanding guest services.*

When we have the desirable quality of goodwill in our own lives, we become a positive force in developing harmony in our staff relationships. Our consideration and support encourage others to behave in a manner that also brings about their best qualities. Not only do we assist in bringing out positive attributes, but we will hopefully be an influence in motivating our entire golf staff to show goodwill. This is because goodwill always has a tendency to spread. *When we develop better skills with people, one of the first distinctions will be in how others begin to treat us differently.* Without realizing it, the goodwill that we have given out to our guests has returned back to us.

Quality #6
Hospitality

Everyone responds positively when they feel welcomed. This is because it makes them feel included as well as accepted. Those who are excellent in the area of people skills and serving others consistently have the ability to show hospitality. These people also make others feel important simply because of the way they have treated them in a highly respectful manner. *Exceptional service is having the ability to make our guests feel like VIP's. When a person is warmly received, it makes him or her also feel a sense of acceptance.* This is exactly what being hospitable does. It gives people a positive feeling of security and a sense of belonging. Not only is this a key to better relationships, but it also creates outstanding Golf Club services.

If we are to succeed in building a strong service team at our club, we must make hospitality a part of our training. *By getting into the habit of making those around us feel welcomed, we not only will see our people skills improving, but we will find that our guests will be more drawn by our welcoming disposition.*

Quality #7
Listening

Listening is one of the best gifts that we can give to others. Not only are we showing consideration, but we are also conveying an attitude of respect. *Healthy relationships happen when people listen to each other.* This virtue is also a key element if we are to improve in the area of guest service at our Golf Club. Everyone likes to be listened to. This is because it gives them the opportunity to open up and share what is on their mind. *When we give our undivided attention, it shows others that we feel that what they are saying is important.* Our people skills instantly improve because of the respect that is conveyed during the act of listening.

It becomes difficult to maintain healthy relationships when we have poor listening skills. This is because a relationship cannot flourish without clear communication. When we listen well, not only are we showing others that we possess great communication skills, but we are also showing excellent service by the respect conveyed through a listening ear.

Quality #8
Patience

There is something about being in the presence of a person who is patient with us. It is a virtue that is welcomed by all. *This is because we see the need for it in our own lives, and are continually confronted with situations that call for patience.* Whether it comes in the form of needing fortitude with another person, or simply waiting for something to arrive, this virtue is constantly being exercised in each of our lives.

Developing great guest services also takes patience. One day we may feel that we have splendid patience with others, and then all of a sudden a new situation arises that may test our patience. But if we are to succeed in our relationships, we must press on in our quest to consistently be patient with others. In essence, we want to show the same kind of patience that we may need from time to time.

The best way to build this virtue into our lives is to learn to be patient during the moments in our lives that call for patience. It is when we are in the midst of having our patience tried that we are actually learning to be more patient. In other words, we learn to be patient during those times when our patience seems to be stretched to the limit. After we have patiently endured, we will soon discover a deeper level in our patience with others. Not only will our relationships improve, but our service will be given higher marks by our guests.

Quality #9
Service mentality

Finally, when we enjoy serving, we are in effect showing an unselfish attitude. This quality is attractive in that it expresses that our focus is on others. People quickly take notice when we live an unselfish lifestyle by the service mentality that we display. *It also attracts because others recognize that our lives are marked with the quality of having a willingness to serve.*

Having a servant's attitude is being aware of others' needs. It is looking beyond ourselves and our own desires and seeking ways to assist the guests who patronize our Golf Club. *We show by our willingness to help that we care.* Instead of seeking to do the minimal requirements for our guests, we live with the mentality to seek out ways to make their visit as enjoyable as possible.

One of the key components of being able to offer exceptional guest service is to look beyond ourselves and see the needs of others. It is being willing to serve without a thought of what is in it for us. In other words, we live with the mindset that moves outside of ourselves and to the needs of those around us.

A closing thought…

As we come to a close, may we see serving others as a privilege that will consistently bring out the best in our service team. Not only will we become more fulfilled in our daily responsibilities with those that we have the privilege to serve, but we will also take on a reputation as an excellent first-class Golf Club operation.

About the Author

Since 1975 Cary has personally served over 100,000 guests. During these years he has observed and learned what truly brings guests back. Cary's zeal to find out what guests want has been his driving passion in building a successful career as a Golf Professional.

After receiving a B.A. at the University of Michigan and an M.A. at Eastern Michigan University, Cary then went on to receive his PGA Membership and become an award-winning Head Professional at various clubs in the Midwest.

Cary's expertise is in the area of guest service. Having authored various books on the subject, Cary has an experienced understanding of how to win the guest and exceed his or her expectations.

Because of his vast experience in providing over 30 years of personal service to a wide variety of guests, Cary is well qualified to coach others in what guests are really looking for when they make contact with a business.

Outside of his enthusiasm for teaching others the real reasons why guests return, Cary enjoys time with his wife Carol and their three children, Sara, Nathan, and Hanna.

Service That Attracts Seminars™

Helping America Serve Better

We offer guest service seminars to fit your needs for understanding why guests return. The insightful workshops are for both management and employees and are intended to build five-star service within your Golf Club.

We offer Keynote Speaking, and on-site *Service That Attracts Seminars*™ that are available for the establishment that is looking to improve on customer service. The fun and interactive presentation will motivate each team member to *want to serve their guests more effectively.* Along with addressing why guests return, we will also explore *why guests choose not to return.*

If you are looking for a life-changing seminar of insightful applications for your Golf Club, the workshops may be exactly what you are looking for. The positive changes will be felt immediately! More information can be found at:

www.carycavittconsulting.com

ഇരു

Service Starts With a Smile looks at 69 ways to bring customers back time and again. It really comes down to treating others the way that we would like to be treated. The tips are simple reminders of the importance of showing each customer consideration and respect. Each thought has stood the test of time and will continue to work for any type of organization that is looking to improve on customer service and gain repeat customers.

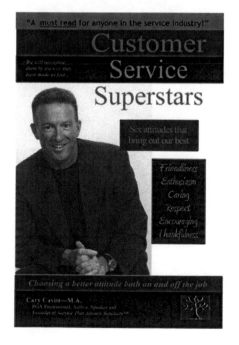

ഇരു

Customer Service Superstars looks at the six most important attitudes that will influence every aspect of our service. By understanding and improving on these highly regarded traits, our service as well as our relationships will begin to change for the better. In the end, we will discover that our relationships both on and off the job are largely determined by our attitudes.

ℰℐℂℬ

Five-Star Service focuses on what great service looks like and how to consistently offer it. The book is broken down into sixteen questions pertaining to customer service. The answers are simple and to the point and are a great reference and reminder of what it takes to bring about five-star service to our customers.

ℰℐℂℬ

Winning the Customer offers insights into the mind of the customer and how to understand their seventeen most important needs. We will discover that every customer is measuring our service based on how well we have met these needs. Everything from how happy we are to serve them to making them feel accepted will ultimately determine whether or not they become loyal.

ဆာ

Luxury Service looks at what it really takes to deliver exceptional service. We will learn that great service can only happen when we serve with the *five key mindsets* discussed throughout the pages. Whether your establishment is an exclusive resort on an island or a local business in your community, *Luxury Service* will clearly explain how to create service that goes above and beyond what your client expected.

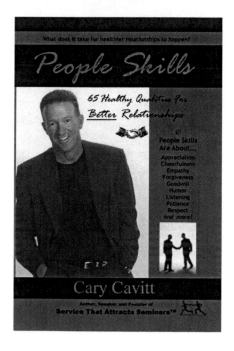

ဆာ

Healthy relationships result when we develop healthy inner qualities. In *People Skills* we will learn that the more inner virtues we possess, the better our relationships will be. We will also find our relationships improving as we begin to build the sixty-five qualities discussed into our lives. In the end, we will discover that positive changes both in our service and relationships will improve for the better.

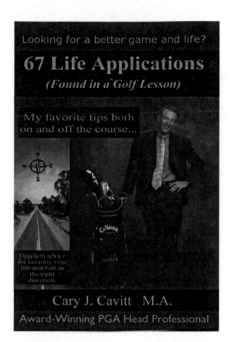

Looking for a better game and life?

67 Life Applications
(Found in a Golf Lesson)

My favorite tips both on and off the course...

Timeless advice for keeping your life and ball in the right direction.

Cary J. Cavitt   M.A.

Award-Winning PGA Head Professional

ॐ∫ॐ

In *67 Life Applications (Found in a Golf Lesson)* we will discover that one simple golf tip can instantly make an improvement in our game. Life is the same way. We hear a quote or are given some sound advice and begin making positive changes. My hope is that each reader will finish this short book and walk away with one or two thoughts that will not only improve their golf game, but also their outlook on life.